The Christmas Truce Book Two

Jesse's Journal

To Hilda

all my best

[signature]

Special thanks to everyone who helped bring this to
completion.

Chapter One

It was white and cold outside the house. Light from the kitchen and great room spilled from the windows accentuating the white powder accumulating on the ridge with its customary peaceful beauty. Maggie shivered every time she looked out even though the softly falling snow brightened her somewhat subdued spirit. She and her siblings were talking softly around the tree, its lights and tinsel glittering. Occasionally they laughed, but she noticed in her childlike way that her aunts and uncles were not as joyful and she wondered whether it had anything to do with the earlier conversations with her mom and dad about life and death, earlier in the week.

***

Down the hall, her grandfather Jesse lay in his bed barely conscious. He muttered now and again trying to respond to the muffled voices coming through the door, words he thought were meant for him. He was alone, he was dying and—though he'd never want his children to know it—he was afraid. Gruff and gritty to the end, too weak to call or even speak, yet too proud to admit his fear had he the strength. He lay there waiting for the end of the struggle, longing for the cessation of pain. Yet dreading it as well. There were things he needed to say, wanted to. The earlier troubling event had prevented that. He knew these were his last moments, still he struggled against the final breath, his heart bursting with regret.

Then he heard the door creak open. His eyelids fluttered as a sliver of light streaked briefly across the room. Not nearly enough time for him to strain his weary eyes open; then darkness again and si… *Wait. What's that?* Someone shuffling across the room. *Who? Who is it?*

"Dad, it's me. It's Tommy."

Tommy? Oh Tommy. I'm sorry son. Jesse thought he'd spoken, but he was far too weak. *I'm so sorry. Can you hear me son? Why don't you answer me?* His own thoughts were quite distinct, he heard them clearly. But life had already left his vocal cords. He lay helplessly in the darkness as his son did the talking.

"John said you were asking about us. Lana and I went to a Christmas Eve service at the church of one of my childhood friends. Remember Sherry? I crashed my bike in front of her house the first time I saw her jumping and yelling my name and walked all the way home crying."

Tommy chuckled in recounting the event, and it pierced Jesse's heart. To laugh; just once more to laugh with this boy. They had done so little laughing together.

"Anyway, she invited us to their Christmas Eve service tonight," Tommy continued. "I know you were never much on that kind of thing."

Jesse felt a hand brushing back the thin, gray hair on his brow. He'd felt it a day earlier. The same hand, the identical voice, the unchanged anguish. As a tear puddled near his nose, Tommy spoke on.

"The service was very nice, especially with the snow. It's snowing right now, so the kids will have a white Christmas. For my kids, it'll be their first. What I wanted to say Dad is that...I'm—I'm sorry. I'm so sorry."

Me too son, Jesse tried to cry, *me too.*

"I'm sorry for today and the argument we had—for *all* the arguments we've had. I'm sorry I wasn't a worthier son. I feel so bad for blaming you for not being a better dad to me or a loving husband to Mom. I regret that somewhere along the line we stopped being friends. I'm sorry my pride got in the way.

"I've blamed you for a lot of things. They were my fault as much as yours, maybe more so. I guess you were right. Some things just don't work out the way you hope or expect. Things do come at you out of the dark and—I wasn't prepared for them."

Eyes still closed, Jesse strained to listen. The words were becoming garbled, frequently interrupted by sniffling.

"I always thought you'd failed me, but I know now you didn't. I just wish I could've seen it earlier. I'm sorry my children haven't known you because of my anger. Maybe there could've been other white Christmases."

Tommy stopped speaking for a time to Jesse's dismay. *Tommy? Tommy, are you there? Son?*

"I have to say good-bye now, Dad. But before I go, I need to say this; I've asked God to forgive me, and now I need to ask the same of you. I forgive you, Dad, and I hope if you can hear me, that you'll forgive me too."

Forgive? Oh yes, dear God forgive me! Forgive me Tommy! A lump rose in Jesse's throat. He heard the boy shuffling away. *Tommy!*

"Tommy."

He'd spoken. His desperate anguish had grown until the spasms in his chest gushed forth enough air to mutter softly. But there was no response. *Was he gone already? Dear God don't let it be too late. Please God...*

"Tommy!"

He strained so hard to speak he couldn't hear the usual noises in the room. Suddenly a hand clasped his. Oh, how he wished he could look upon his son, but there was no strength. He felt himself grow faint, the room began to swirl.

Dear God, let him find them. Please let him find...

The last sound he heard was his son weeping in the darkness.

Chapter Two

Tommy pushed away from the table eleven months later and made his way to the living room. They'd just finished their Thanksgiving dinner and as usual, for the holiday, he'd overeaten. The children ran off into another room to watch one of their favorite Christmas movies as his wife Lana sat down next to him. She pulled her legs up under her after sipping her decaf.

"Another fantastic dinner honey." He groaned in discomfort and patted his belly. "Thanks so much. I surely should get up and work some of this off this evening."

Lana laughed. "You've been saying that for ten years now and you never do it. We both know you'll set right there and sleep most of the evening. But if you want something to do I could use some help with the dishes."

Tommy feigned a snore and Lana poked him in the ribs. He chuckled and sat up straight. "I suppose that's the least I can do, isn't it?"

"It certainly is. But … let's talk first. You were a bit broken up while we were sharing our thanks before dinner." She stroked his hair softly. "Can I ask why?"

The smile disappeared, his gut tightened as he struggled to find the words. "Honey?" Lana pressed. He shifted positions and gazed at the ceiling for a moment while she waited. "I'm still struggling with Dad's death, I guess. Even though it's been almost a year now, I'm still uneasy about it."

"Really? How long have you been feeling this way?" She eased closer to him and laid her arm around his shoulders. "Ever since last Christmas?"

"No…not that long. A couple of weeks, perhaps. But it's getting harder to dismiss the feelings as the holidays draw closer."

"I'm sure that's normal for anyone who's lost a loved one during the holiday season." She sipped some coffee watching for his response.

He shook his head. "It's more than that I think. You know, last year Christmas was almost ruined by my anger. Now this year it seems my regrets are clouding it."

"In what way?" She rubbed his neck and shoulders. He appreciated the effort yet it didn't help relieve the tension. Tommy stood, stretched, then dragged himself over to the window and looked out at the gathering dusk. "I…uh, I'm just wondering whether he—whether Dad made things right with God."

"Right with God?" She lowered her cup.

"Yes. I know *we* were reconciled at that moment. But did he have time to—did he want to—." Tommy couldn't continue.

"I don't know," Lana replied softly. "I don't guess we'll ever be sure about that, until that day when we hope to be reunited. But I know dwelling on regrets won't give you the answer."

He turned towards her and crossed his arms; his head bowed. He shuffled his feet and sighed. "You're right of course, but in my defense I don't think it's just regret that's weighing on me."

Lana rose and walked into the kitchen to begin gathering the dishes. Tommy followed and turned on the water to fill the sink. "What else is bothering you then?"

"Well…" He hesitated. Lana stopped what she was doing and turned to him.

"Go on Tommy. Get it out in the open."

"You know I was sincere when I told Dad that I forgave him right?" She nodded. "And you know that I was and am more than willing to admit how I failed him." She nodded again then turned back to the dishes as he continued.

"I've…uh, been wondering…what made him the way he was. Why did it seem he didn't like me, his own son? What happened to make him so cold and distant? Remember the baseball story I told you I'd shared with Naismith? What transpired in Dad's life that made him so incapable of loving his son openly and freely? Or was he always that way?" Tommy flopped down at the table as Lana drained the sink. She refilled her coffee and sat down near him.

"Why was there such a hardness between us?"

"I don't know Tommy. I didn't realize it was that important to you. How long have you been thinking about that?"

"A lot longer than a few months—off and on for years, I guess. But lately it seems to be especially on my mind. I think that's one of the regrets I have. If I hadn't been so prideful and stubborn, so angry, maybe I could have learned the answers before he died."

"Perhaps, but I don't know how you'd find out something like that now. Do you think Dina and John could help?"

"Maybe. However, I've got a sneaking hunch that what I'm really looking for is further back in his history. Before we came into the picture, maybe even before Mom was in his life."

"It won't hurt to ask them would it? Why not give them a call?"

"No, I guess not. But you know how I prefer to do things in person. I can do it next month when we go home for...Christmas. Home for Christmas. I'm also nervous about going back there again. Almost as reluctant as I was last year. I wonder why?" He gazed at her innocently, and she smiled.

"I'm sure there are lots of reasons connected to that—your continued estrangement from John, the bitter memories of your dad; the reality that the house will be sold after this Christmas, once and for all severing your connection with your childhood and, memories of your mom. That's a big step."

She chuckled and Tommy wondered about this sudden change in mood. "What's funny about that?"

"I just remembered something from *my* childhood. When I was a little girl, we often moved. I distinctly recall a little ritual I had. I'd walk through each room and think about things that had happened in that house."

"Seriously?" He leaned closer, trying to picture the scene in his mind. "I never knew that about you."

She nodded. "Oh yes. Odd how it came back to me just now. I suppose we've never had a chance to talk about it before. It's as clear as crystal. I would walk into each room and think about something that had happened there. Christmases, or birthdays, or some other trivial thought. And then I'd go outside and look at the window of my room and say good-bye, so to speak."

Tommy felt a warm sensation inside and bowed. "There will be some house parting sorrow in the weeks ahead I suppose. I never thought of it that way. How old were you when this ritual ceased?"

She handed him a dish to dry, and stared off into space for a moment. "I'd say till I was in my mid-teens. That's the last time we moved. I don't know if that's what you're feeling or not, but I could understand if you were. You know all the things we cling to through life—photos, souvenirs, little tokens of remembrance—they're all connections to the past bringing back a smell, a sensation. Houses do that as well. And even though there were painful memories for you in that house, there were good ones also, especially in regards to your mom. Once you say good-bye to that house, the memories are all you have left, and… well, it's a final reminder that you can't go back, that a chapter of the book of your life is closed forever."

He nodded before breaking into a chuckle. "Okay, thanks Lana for brightening our holiday spirit with those melancholy sentiments. Merry Christmas Debbie Downer!"

They laughed together for a moment and hugged each other but when the humor had passed, she sensed him becoming subdued again.

"Maybe you're right after all. It's something to think about over the next weeks. But before I say goodbye to the old place once and for all I sure wish it would give up some of its secrets about Dad. I'd love for that to happen."

Chapter Three

"Yes, Jeanette," Tommy replied to the intercom voice of his secretary two weeks later. He'd been looking over some Christmas cards from clients.

"There's a man here who'd like to see you, Mr. Howell. He doesn't have an appointment, but he says it's very important."

Tommy never averted his attention from the holiday wishes before him, pushing aside for the moment highlighted business papers. "In regards to what?"

"He says it's in connection to your father's

estate."

Tommy stopped and looked up. His mind instantly filled with the thoughts and conversation he and Lana had shared Thanksgiving night.

"Mr. Howell?" Jeanette inquired after a moment of delay.

"Yes…yes, send him in." He stood and moved to the door. Opening it he felt a sense of familiarity as the man approached. "Come in." Tommy shook his hand then motioned him toward a chair. The man paced over quickly then sat down, a unique wooden box situated in his lap. "How may I help you, Mr?"

"Dorian. Richard Dorian."

"Dorian? Now why does that name sound familiar?" Tommy studied the man, trying to place his face with his name.

"You won't recognize me, Mr. Howell; we've never met. You may be familiar with my name because I purchased a number of your father's household furnishings, those you'd decided to sell, at the auction last spring. You children had to sign off on the purchase, so that's probably where you've heard the name."

Tommy sat back in his chair. "Ah. Okay, that's probably correct. Well then, how can I help you Mr. Dorian."

"Richard, please."

"All right, how can I assist you, Richard?" He smiled mischievously. "I'm afraid we can't take returns of the merchandise."

Richard chuckled. "No, no returns, Mr. Howell. But I did find this container in one of the old chests." He lifted the box from his lap and laid it on Tommy's desk. It was about the length of and twice the width of a shoebox, with artistic carvings on its top and sides. "I felt certain it might be of value to the family. Do you recognize it?"

Tommy shrugged. "Never seen it before in my life. You needn't have gone to all the trouble to return it. It's probably just on old keepsake my father never told us about. That wasn't unusual with him."

Mr. Dorian shook his head. "I brought it to *you*, for one thing, because I happened to be passing through Charleston on a business trip." He pushed the box toward Tommy.

Tommy crossed his arms on the desk before him and stared at it. "You said 'for one thing.' Was there another reason?"

"It wasn't only the box I was concerned to return, Mr. Howell. It's what's inside."

"In it?" Tommy stared as Richard reached up, undid the latch and flipped open the lid, revealing a menagerie of papers and documents. "What in the world?" Tommy ran his fingers across the edges and pulled a small photo from the case. He sat quietly taking in the scene of a young couple.

"Hmmm, that certainly looks like Mom and Dad," he mused aloud. "But like the box, I've never seen it. You say it was with the furniture?"

"Yes sir. Frankly I'm not sure how it was missed in the inventory process, but I felt certain that it was an oversight." Richard leaned back now in his chair. "I hope you don't mind sir but I did scan the material slightly. I wanted to make sure it was important enough to return, and it seemed to me that it was."

Tommy leafed through the papers as Mr. Dorian talked, but saw nothing of consequence.

"Well. I appreciate you bringing it by, Richard, but you might have mailed the contents easier and kept the box for yourself. Of course if you'd like I can take the documents and let you retain the object." Tommy reached out to remove the documents.

"I couldn't do that sir," Richard replied resolutely. Tommy paused and turned to his visitor.

"And why not?"

"Because of this, Mr. Howell." Richard pointed to a small engraving inside the lid. "That's my second reason for bringing it to *you*."

Tommy looked closely, and his mouth eased open.

For Tommy, it read.

Tommy sat silently puzzling over the inscription as Richard sat back again. Tommy pushed away from the desk, rose, and walked to the window. He stared out over the harbor for a moment, then pulled his handkerchief out and cleaned his reading glasses. In reality, he was hiding a small tear. He hesitated to believe this was related to he and Lana's discussion Thanksgiving evening. He turned to his guest.

"It must be a different Tommy." He chortled. "I tell you I've never seen it before. Why would Dad have bought an engraved box that he never told me about?"

"Perhaps…he uh…meant to tell you before he died."

Tommy studied his visitor for a moment, possessed with a strange feeling that Dorian was being a tad mysterious.

"That's possible…I suppose. He was very ill in the end, and we didn't…" He turned again to the window and brought the handkerchief to his face. He cleared his throat. "We didn't get to talk much before the…uh...before the end."

"Then it's fortunate I brought it to your attention." Richard stood to his feet. "Since I'm sure you'll now want to retain it, I will be going."

Tommy turned back to him. "Yes, yes it was very good of you to do so. I…uh…I appreciate it. Is there anything else I can do for you Richard?"

"Just one other question, Mr. Howell. When is the final sale of the property to take place?"

"At the first of the year. We're going to spend one more Christmas there, our families that is. One more Christmas at home before we let it go." He couldn't prevent his eyes from misting up. "Are you…ahem, would you be interested?"

"I'm certainly interested in the rest of the furnishings. I've a couple other business issues to resolve before I know whether I'll have the capital to pursue the entire estate, but it's been on my mind." Tommy walked with him toward Jeanette's desk.

"It's a beautiful location as you know, and will make someone a great home for raising a family." Tommy's voice trembled involuntarily as he spoke.

"Yes," Richard replied. "I fully agree. I'd imagine letting go of the place would cause a little stress at this time of year, the memories and all that."

"I suppose so," Tommy whispered. So many of his years there had been turbulent, still he felt very melancholy about the possibility of the house being beyond his reach forever. And the sensation puzzled him.

"Maybe you'll find something in the box to help you cope with the stress of letting go."

Tommy stopped suddenly as they reached Jeanette's desk. He'd thought to walk his visitor to the elevator, until Richard's comment. There was that feeling again, as if his guest was leaving something unsaid. That sense of familiarity that lingered as they shook hands. But Tommy dismissed it.

It's just a box, sheer coincidence that can't possibility tell me anything about Dad.

"Well thanks again for your consideration in bringing the box by. Merry Christmas!"

"Merry Christmas to you," Richard replied as he smiled first at Tommy, then Jeanette, before moving to the elevator. Tommy watched him step on, then returned to his office.

***

Lana met Tommy at the door that evening. She'd looked out the window at his usual time and saw him making his way toward the house arms loaded with briefcases and file folders. She swung the door open just as he reached the threshold.

"Good evening. What in the world are you carrying? Don't you know this week is a holiday week? You're supposed to be off work." She smiled as she took some of the bags and folders from his hand.

"The key phrase there is 'supposed to be' off. I'm sorry to ruin your plans for this evening, but I must get some of this work done before we go away. You'll have to do that last minute shopping tonight without me."

Lana smirked. "What a relief."

Like everything else about Christmas, and unlike most men, Tommy loved those holiday shopping excursions, almost too much. Lana usually had to harp about his spending which tended to dampen the spirit of the season.

"Aw, that's too bad." Lana laughed. Her eyes twinkled, and her snowy teeth beamed from a broad smile.

"Yea, I can see how broken up you are about it." Tommy began laying the bundles on the table.

"So, other than your slave labor, how did your day—what in the world is that?"

She grabbed the box from his hand and began turning it and studying the various engravings. "This is very fine Native American craftsmanship. Where'd you get it? Is it a present?" She walked into the living room and set it on the coffee table as Tommy followed.

"To answer your question my day went pretty smoothly, nothing out of the ordinary until late this afternoon when that appeared on my desk."

Lana looked at him quizzically, and he took the next few moments recounting his encounter with Richard Dorian.

"Why didn't he just Fed-Ex the documents?"

"I had the same question. Look." Tommy reached down flipped open the lid and pointed to the engraving. "That's why."

"Whoa." Lana's eyes widened as she turned to her husband. "Now that's a little spooky isn't it? I mean we were just talking about this the other week and presto a guy brings you an engraved box. What did you tell him?" She leafed through the papers as he spoke.

"I told him it must be a different Tommy. I'm sure it's just an odd coincidence. Dad probably picked it up somewhere, began using it for storage of trivialities, and had no idea it even had an engraving."

Lana sat back and exhaled heavily. "Yes…it could be a coincidence. But if so, it's a strange one. Have you studied the contents?"

"No, I haven't," Tommy called behind him as he went into the kitchen for a drink. "Not in any detail at least. I glanced through it and then set it aside, too much on my plate today, and tonight.

"Well, it might be interesting when you get a chance. I'll go finish dinner." Lana rose and went to the kitchen while Tommy sat down and stared at the box. A moment later the children bounded into the room, and they had their daily exchange about the day. Lana came in and placed the box out of the way on a china hutch.

Chapter Four

"Let's go kids," Lana called as she stuffed the last of the presents into the back of the van a week later. "We've got a six-hour drive and your father wants to be there in time to get a good fire going." The boys piled in, and Maggie crawled across them to her seat and buckled in.

"Everybody ready?" Tommy drew the front door shut and jiggled the knob. He looked toward the car and scratched his head, took a step or two, then hesitated again.

"What did you forget?" Lana smiled. This was the usual routine. He shrugged and continued on. "All set everyone?" He pulled the van door tight, buckled up and slipped the gear selector to Drive.

"I hope we don't get boxed in by traffic on the interstate," Lana mused as she flipped through the pages of a magazine.

Screech! The tires squealed on the pavement. The children looked around wide-eyed as Lana regained her composure.

"What in the world are you doing?" She glared at Tommy. "What's wrong?"

"'Boxed in', that's what. I just remembered something we probably want to take along." He whipped the van around at the end of a cul-de-sac and sped back toward the house.

"Come again."

"I forgot the chest Mr. Dorian brought me." He pulled up to the house fumbled with the keys and disappeared inside once more. In a minute, he returned with the ornate carved container which had lain on the hutch mostly neglected for the past week. Lana took it from his hands as he climbed into the van.

"I'd almost forgotten about this as well, Tommy. It would've been a shame to have left it. I know John and Dina have been waiting to get a look inside."

"John and Dina? How'd they find out about it?" Tommy kept his eyes on the road, as Lana traced the carvings with her finger.

"I posted a photo of it on Facebook last week. Gave them a brief overview of how it came into your possession."

"Did they know anything about it? What'd

they say?" In spite of the fact that he hadn't had time to explore the contents since he brought it home, Tommy couldn't hide his excitement.

"They didn't recognize it either. I didn't tell them about this though." She opened the lid and pointed to the engraving. "I wasn't sure whether you would approve of that, so I left it alone."

"I can't see that it makes any difference. I need to fill up with gas before we go any farther." He pulled into a convenience station and set about the task as the kids fidgeted, and Lana pondered the box.

"Find anything interesting," Tommy asked as he started the van again.

"Hmmm. Maybe. I leafed through the envelopes and papers looking at postmark dates and return addresses for a moment. And then I studied the engraving itself." She rubbed the mark with her index finger.

"And what did you discover?"

"You won't be able to see what I mean because you're driving, but I think the personalized engraving was added sometime after the box was made." She turned it again then flipped the lid several times scrutinizing the exterior carvings with the name.

"And what makes you think that?" Tommy flipped on the blinker and pressed the accelerator as they joined the flow of traffic on the interstate.

"Well…I'm no expert, even though I did minor in native art forms, but it seems to me like a different tool was used on the name engraving. It's not as smooth and flowing as the external carvings." Tommy looked over as Lana pointed out the contrast.

"I can't see that clearly from here. I'll let you drive later, and I'll study it some then. However, it might have a simple explanation."

"Such as?"

"Such as the craftsman not being as adept at carving names."

"No…I don't think so." Lana shook her head firmly.

Tommy chuckled. "And just why not Miss suddenly art expert?"

Lana laughed sarcastically in return while turning the bottom of the box up. "Because …the engraver carved his name in the bottom, see— Jeremiah Youngeagle. The strokes are smooth and flowing like the rest of the box. The interior engraving is rough, with short jagged cuts."

Buuuurump.

"Keep your eyes on the road, please!" Lana cried out as Tommy steered the car off the rumble strip. "You can look at it later."

"Yesss ma'am!" They laughed together for a moment as Lana closed the box and passed it to Danny in the back seat. "Lay this with the other presents darling boy, before your father ruins our Christmas with a hospital stay." Tommy couldn't resist more playful taunting.

"So what do you think you've proven, Sherlock Holmes?"

"That your father might have been the one to make the engraving; which, if true, means it was *meant* for you."

He felt his broad smile fade with her reply. *Meant for me?*

Silence came between them as they whisked along the highway. The children were chattering and watching videos, Lana periodically serving as referee for disputes between them. Tommy was barely conscious of it all. He couldn't put that last phrase of Lana's out of his mind. *Meant for me. Is it possible?*

He swallowed hard. Last year's holiday had forced him to see how unfair he'd been to his father, he thought he was past that now. But…what if the box was meant for him? Could it be that his father had secretly longed to answer all the nagging questions Tommy had about their relationship, but was never given the chance? Tommy was afraid to hope for that.

Three hours later they pulled into a restaurant just south of Charlotte and stretched as the children tumbled out of the van. After being shown to their table and ordering, they made small talk with the children. Lana called Dina to check her and Wayne's progress as Tommy explained to Maggie why there would be no snow on this Christmas trip.

"How are they," Tommy asked when Lana ended the call.

"They're stuck in traffic—an accident just south of Knoxville. They're going to be a little late."

The waitress appeared with their orders, and the next moments were jumbled with getting the children settled.

"How did Dina sound, Lana?"

"Miserable. Snarled on the interstate when you're eight months pregnant is no picnic!"

"Any idea how long they'll be delayed?"

"Not precisely, but Wayne estimates about six more hours before they arrive. One thing is certain, she'll be exhausted."

Tommy nodded. "Gee, I'm sorry for their grief but it'll give me a chance to get a good fire going, and we'll have hot chocolate waiting when they pull in. You can drive when we leave here. Okay?"

Lana agreed, and they finished their meal. Back on the road again the winter sun was drawing near the western horizon. A full stomach and much cooler air near the mountains made Tommy feel lazy and listless. He adjusted the seat to recline a little. The children's voices rose and sank as the two brothers tried to convince hopeful Maggie there would be no snow this year. Tommy dozed off for a half hour or so before Lana roused him once more.

"W-what's wrong?"

"Nothing. I just need some directions here as always. Right or left at this turn?"

"Left." Tommy shook the sleep from his eyes.

"That was a nice little nap you had."

"Yes it was, and I needed it." He rubbed his hands together. "I hope to do a bit more this week next to the wood stove."

Lana smiled. "Have you thought about anything else to do?"

"Not particularly. Just be lazy and enjoy the kids. Maybe we'll go down to see Sherry one day. I mean if she's still working at Sara's Place."

"That will be nice. Anything else?"

Tommy turned to her. "What do you mean anything else? What are you driving at?"

She tipped her head toward the back of the van. "What about the box?" He turned away gazing out the window. "I don't know," he responded softly. "I think we'll have plenty of time to look at it."

"Who is 'we?'" She pulled the van to the side of the road. "You'll need to take over now." They switched places without missing a beat in the conversation.

"What do you mean 'who is we?' John, Dina, and myself. You said they were interested didn't you?" His voice tightened, and he wondered why the idea was irritating.

"Yes they're interested. But the box was meant for you and—"

"Hold on now Lana, that hasn't been determined. It might be meant for me, and it might be pure coincidence. Neither of us has spent any real time looking over the documents. I still say it belonged to another Tommy, and Dad just used it for pure convenience. Until I find something conclusive in it, I will keep on believing that."

She turned toward him and continued softly. "Are you certain that's how you really feel? Is it possible you're afraid you'll find something to rekindle your anger?"

"What? Don't be silly, all that was dealt with last year. Why makes you think that?"

"Your feigned indifference for one thing. At Thanksgiving you were longing to know more. Now a container has arrived that might hold a few answers and you're resistant to the idea of examining it. Most people would be anxious to explore the possibility. Fear or anger seem to be the most likely reasons for your hesitance."

He concentrated on the road without responding. Lana pressed on.

"What would you like to find?"

Tommy shook his head and looked about somewhat perturbed.

"Find? What…what are you talking about?"

"In the box? What would you like to find in the box? What might make you believe your father meant it for you?" She glanced over at him and clicked the seat to its upright position. He sighed deeply.

"I know it's still uncomfortable for you, but you have to consider it," she persisted. "Especially if you want to find the answers we were talking about at Thanksgiving. This can't be mere coincidence, Tommy. I know you haven't had, or taken time to study the contents, but haven't you even thought about it? Maybe the answers are in there."

They pulled to a stop sign just outside Destiny, and Tommy turned to his wife. He looked long and deep into her eyes. He did want to know, longed to believe that beneath his father's rough exterior and abrupt manner was a man who had cared for him. But he'd gotten his hopes up so often only to have them dashed. He was afraid to allow his expectations to be raised again. He couldn't have described it, but there was a wound still healing from that broken promise at the overlook. He reached over and squeezed her hand, a signal to let it lie for a while. When they pulled off, the conversation turned to other things till they neared the house he had called home for so many years.

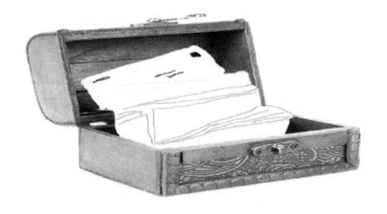

Chapter Five

Lana looked at the clock as car lights pierced the windows. As predicted, it had been about six hours since she'd spoken to Dina on the phone. She watched as Maggie ran out to meet her favorite aunt but Dina was clearly unable to return her Christmas excitement. Her visible fatigue made her abrupt with everyone. Lana was the only one who understood.

"Come in here and sit by the fire, Dina. Tommy has it very warm now. It will help you relax." Lana helped Dina get settled while Tommy went to assist Wayne in unloading their car. "You must be exhausted."

Dina slid onto the couch. "I can't even begin to tell you how exhausted. What a difficult day. Ten hours we've been on that road. Ten! I am beat!"

"Can I get you anything? Are you hungry?" Lana stood near her.

"I'm always hungry, but I can't eat anything heavy this late. Do you have anything light?"

"Actually," Lana began, "we happen to have some salad made. I planned to make a big dish of Lasagna tomorrow, and I prepped the salad tonight. Would you like some?"

"That would do nicely." Dina squirmed in her seat. "Oh, my back."

"I'll bring something for that also," Lana said. She hurried off into the kitchen and busily prepared the salad amid the clinking of plates and glasses.

Wayne flopped down on the couch next to his exhausted wife as Lana brought the food tray.

"How about you Wayne? We have some sloppy Joes left over from earlier."

"Yum!" He jumped up and headed for the kitchen. "I'll serve myself though. You sit down and help the little mother relax."

Tommy followed Wayne leaving the women chattering about pregnancy and other related concerns. A half hour later the cold mountain air began to descend upon the ridge, creeping its way into the house.

"Tommy," Lana called out. "It's getting a little chilly in here."

Tommy came back and stoked the fire as Lana carried in a tray of hot cocoa and sugar cookies. The boys were mumbling in their room down the hall, and Maggie lay curled up next to Dina. Her spirit now revived, she looked across the room.

"Is that it," Dina asked pointing. They all turned toward the small chest.

"Yes," Tommy said softly. "That is the mystery box."

"Bring it over and let me see," Dina requested. Tommy set his cocoa on the stove then moved across the room and picked up the case. He returned, setting it down before Wayne and Dina, who had scooched forward to the edges of their seats.

Wayne traced the carvings with his finger. "Have you examined the documents inside?"

"No, Wayne I haven't. I've uh…been so busy since Mr. Dorian's delivery two weeks ago, I haven't had time." He chuckled, trying to hide his lingering discomfort at what might be found there. "In fact, we almost forgot all about the box this morning. We drove off without it when we first left the house."

Dina flipped open the lid and started pulling papers out and glancing over them. "Do you think we should wait for John to arrive tomorrow before the examination?"

Tommy shrugged. "I don't know. I'm convinced that it'll prove a fruitless search." He pulled out the photo of the couple he thought looked like his mom and dad and showed Dina. "So far this is the only thing I've seen that might be worth something."

"Wait a minute," Dina gasped. "I've seen this somewhere before."

Lana looked at her. "You mean this photo?"

"No, I've never seen the picture. At least I don't remember seeing it. But the scenery, something seems very familiar. Oh, I can't place it."

"You're too tired to think about much now," Wayne offered. "And so am I. Let's dispense with the investigation tonight and just enjoy our cookies and cocoa before hitting the sack."

Tommy closed the lid slowly, his hand lingering on the box's ornamented exterior. He was growing conscious of an urging, a desire to dive in—come what may. He sighed and pushed it away. "I agree with Wayne. We'll have plenty of time over the next week to explore the contents. I seriously doubt it'll take that long."

Tommy sensed Lana looking at him. He returned her glance and nodded. He knew what she was thinking. She'd known him long enough to know he was raring to have a look.

Chapter Six

Tommy jerked awake to the sound of Maggie's jubilant cries.

"Daddy! Daddy! It snowed Daddy. I told you so. Snow fell overnight."

"Huh. What?" Tommy groaned as he looked at the clock. "Maggie do you know what time it is?"

"But I wanted you to see that I was right," she continued without missing a beat. "It snowed just like I said."

Tommy staggered to the window as Lana rolled over and pulled the blankets close. He rubbed his eyes and drew back the curtains.

"See!" Maggie squealed. Tommy let the curtain fall back again and looked at the jubilant child. Indecision rippled through his mind. It wasn't snow, just a very heavy frost. How could he explain that? Before he could think up an answer that wouldn't break her heart, she bounded out of the room to tell her brothers.

"Good. Let them get the blame for once," he mumbled, pulling on his pants and sweater.

"What are you talking about?" Lana murmured from beneath the flannel covering.

"Maggie thought it had snowed, but its only frost. She's gone off to tell the boys. They'll set her straight."

"Are you getting up then?"

Tommy turned toward the clock which read seven-thirty, then pulled the blankets farther up on his wife. "Might as well. Need to get the fire going anyway, and some coffee."

"Yes, yes you do that," Lana purred. "I'll see you this afternoon."

Tommy chuckled then treaded softly to the hall pulling the door shut behind him. He stopped at the stove first. Some embers still burning from that log he'd thrown in around three. A quick stirring of the coals, a few pieces of kindling, and the fire leapt to life again. In moments, the metal was popping and expanding as the wood crackled within. A minute or two afterwards he was sitting there sipping on his coffee and nipping at a sweet roll they'd brought along for this purpose. But the serenity was broken as Maggie slumped in from the hallway.

"What's wrong Magpie?" He fully understood the reason for her sullen expression.

"Danny and T.J. called me stupid for saying that it snowed. They say it isn't snow Daddy. What do you say?"

"Hmmm…" He pulled her up into his lap in preparation for the letdown. "It is snow in a way." Her eyes began to light up again and he hated to spoil her enthusiasm. "But… it's not the kind of snow you were hoping for. It's made of the same thing, water and cold air, but you can't make snowmen or snowballs, and it won't stay nearly long enough for sledding. In fact, if you look now you can see the sun is already melting it off the grass."

Maggie strained up in his lap where she could see through the window, her enthusiastic smile quickly replaced by an equally attractive pout. She sat for a while in his lap. All was quiet except for the expanding metal of the stove.

"Would you like to go back to bed," he asked as she yawned for the third time. "You were up mighty early."

"No, but could I have a bowl of cereal?" She slid down and motioned toward the kitchen.

"Of course. Let's go."

He got her settled, refilled his coffee and left her looking dreamily through a toy magazine as she ate. He threw another piece of wood in the stove then sat down gazing over at the box. Lana was right in her assessment last night. He was anxious to study the contents, to see whether it answered any of the questions he had about his father. Curiosity was quickly replacing any fear he had of being disappointed.

John and Sally aren't due until late this afternoon. What would it hurt to take a look now? He started to rise.

"Can a fat, pregnant lady find some place to sit around here?" Dina came abruptly into the room, and Tommy jumped up to help make his sister comfortable on the couch.

"Take my seat. Would you like some coffee?"

"Yes but put some extra creamer in it. I've been having a lot of heartburn lately."

Tommy rushed off, returning in a moment with her mixture and a refill of his own followed by Maggie. Dina breathed in the aroma from the flavored creamer a moment then took a sip as Maggie climbed up beside her. Tommy tossed another piece of wood in the stove and took a seat across from his sister.

"So brother, what have you been doing this morning?"

"Trying to wake up mostly. Magpie here got us up early because she thought the frost was snow. We've had a time convincing her there would be none this year. I think I'm still half asleep."

Dina looked about the room while caressing Maggie's hair with one hand and holding her coffee with the other. "It's hard to believe it's the last time we'll ever gather here for Christmas or anything else. What do you think you'll miss most about this place?"

"I haven't thought much on that. My anger with dad kept me from allowing myself to think of all the positive memories that were made here. I suppose I've got a lot of catching up to do before we say good-bye to the old place. It's something we all have to do sometimes. Say goodbye once and for all."

"We'll have to try getting together at our various homes instead if we're to spend Christmas together." Dina squirmed as if trying to get comfortable.

"I hope you don't mind me saying so," Tommy began, "but you look miserable."

"I am miserable. Just six more weeks are all we have left to wait. Thank God!" They laughed together for a moment as Dina continued to look for a comfortable spot in the couch and Tommy urged Maggie to come sit in his lap to relieve Dina.

"I'm afraid we'll have trouble keeping Maggie happy with Charleston Christmases. Last year's white Christmas put a taste in her mouth that may not be satisfied anytime soon, if ever."

Dina chuckled. "Isn't it amazing how much snow is a part of Christmas? Most people never see a white Christmas. How many did we see in all our years? Two or three?"

"According to John, it was five." Tommy looked around to see a bleary-eyed, unshaven Wayne enter the room. He moved to the back of the couch and gave Dina a brief shoulder rub as he continued. "We discussed that last year after the funeral. He remembered only five."

"It seems like more," Dina mused. "Don't you think Tommy?"

"What? Oh... oh, yeah. It does seem like more." Tommy's attention had started to drift away from the discussion. He was gazing intently on the box. "We're fortunate though to have had that many considering where we are."

"In spite of what you said last night," Wayne began, "I suppose you're anxious to go through the box's documents."

Tommy shrugged. "To be honest, I'm not sure how I feel. Lana and I were talking on Thanksgiving evening about some ongoing questions regarding Dad and me. She seems to think some of the answers might be in there. I'm afraid to get my hopes up about that. And," he said as he rose and walked over to it, "I really can't see how there could be. It's not as if he left a diary for me to read. That kind of stuff doesn't happen in real life."

"We'll know soon enough," Lana said as she entered the room looking down at her phone. "I just got a text from Sally. They expect to be here around noon, ahead of schedule. There'll be too much to do getting settled this afternoon but perhaps you might get your first glimpse after supper."

Tommy felt his chest tighten. He wanted to look but resisted out of an attempt to be respectful to John as the oldest. *Tonight, Dad...tonight*

Lana and Wayne moved into the kitchen to get breakfast started and Dina did her best to cheer up Maggie. Tommy puttered most of the morning with one-thing and then another. Stacking some wood on the porch, settling disputes with Danny and T.J., answering Maggie's persistent "'what if's'" regarding the possibility of snow. And he was working very hard to keep from expecting too much from the box and what might be in the letters and documents it held. He was scared, terribly afraid to get his hopes too high, only to have them dashed. Try as he might he couldn't suppress his growing anticipation. He wished John and Sally would come on and arrive so they could get it over with. He wished now he'd paid more attention to it over the last two weeks. At last he decided he was going for a walk.

***

A little later, Lana walked out on the porch to bask for a moment in the warm sun. She watched her husband as he shuffled along the drive, gravel crunching under his feet. His head was down, lips moving, she knew he was having a private conversation, wrestling with the feelings that were growing inside. He disappeared from her sight for a few minutes around a bend in the drive and then reappeared along the edge of the woods. She followed his movements till he came to a spot about 50 yards from the house. She watched him stop there; arms crossed, his head bowed to the ground. Occasionally he nodded, and his odd mannerisms at last got the best of her.

"Tommy," she called out. "What are you doing honey?"

He turned toward her with a sheepish grin, then began walking to the porch. She leaned against a post as he neared her. "What were you doing out there?"

"Remembering Patches." He slid onto a porch swing, and she joined him, pulling the sweater higher up on her neck.

"Patches?"

"One of my favorite dogs. Dina and I were talking this morning, along the same lines as you and I on our drive up yesterday. She asked what I was going to miss most about the place. I was thinking about that as I walked, and I remembered Patches. That's where we buried her when she died." He tipped his head toward the spot where he'd been standing.

Lana smiled. Thirteen years together and another tidbit of information she'd never known.

"What kind of dog was she?"

"A cross between a black lab and a border collie. She never met a stranger. We used to kid mom about how Patches smiled. Mom never believed it, but it was true." He looked down now, apparently lost in the recollection. "I have to admit I think about her now and again, Patches, I mean. I guess that will end with our goodbyes to this place, as well."

She rubbed his shoulders. "Yes, I suppose it will." She didn't like the tone in his voice, too melancholy. He was slipping into a despondent mood with all the talk about leaving things behind and the emotional uncertainty of what was in the box. He needed something to distract his mind.

"Listen, there are a few more things I need for supper this evening. Could you run into town and get them?"

"Sure. What was it?"

"Garlic toast mainly, but there are a few other things. Do you mind?"

"Would it matter?" He snickered. She shook her head then headed inside to get the list.

When she returned she handed it to him. "Here you go. Oh, and by the way, since you have time, why not stop by and see about Sherry?"

Lana noticed his countenance change. She hoped Sherry would be there and that she could lift his spirits as only friends can do.

Chapter Seven

Tommy pulled his van to a stop on Main Street a little while later. He wasn't familiar with her address so began looking for Sherry at Sara's Place. Climbing out of the van and looking up he saw that the old restaurant sign was gone, replaced by one that read, "Sherry's Plate."

"Well, I'll be. Is it possible?" Inside a moment later his suspicions were confirmed. Across the room, Sherry stood chatting with some customers, no longer clad in a waitress's uniform but in a pant suit. He hardly recognized her. Then she turned to give instructions to the cook. She seemed different than a year earlier—healthier, happier, more confident. Tommy felt a swell of exhilaration that the bitterness of life had left her for a time at least. His joy was compounded when she looked up to see him leaning against the counter. Her eyes brightened even more as she rushed over with a broad grin.

"Tommy."

"Sherry. Look at you." He gave her a hug, and she led him to a booth where both slid in. "It looks like some changes have been going on around here."

"A few. So what do you think? Would you have ever believed it? Me— a restaurant owner?"

"It seems to fit you somehow. How did it happen? When?"

"Just last month. The Clines decided a while back that they'd been in the business long enough and started talking about selling out. I inherited a little money last spring from an uncle, and I thought, why not me? I have to admit I was very nervous about the responsibility, but as it turns out I love it, and, for the moment at least, I seem to be good at it. I love everything about it."

"I can tell." Tommy laughed. "You're beaming. It's quite a contrast from last Christmas. You look so much happier."

"I am," she replied in a somewhat more subdued tone. "I think I have you to thank for it."

"Me?" Tommy exclaimed. "What did I do?"

"You helped me release some things. When you sent that letter last January telling me about how you were able to let go regarding your dad, it made me think."

"But it was you who pushed me," he protested.

"Yes, I know. It must've been one of those 'do as I say not as I do' moments. I sat down looked myself in the eye and realized I wasn't 'practicing what I preached' so to speak. I forgave myself for my perceived failure toward Mom, and things have been looking up ever since. But you, what are you doing here?"

"One more Christmas at home." His voice trailed off despite the effort to prevent it from doing so. "Dad's house, and the remaining furniture, goes up for sale at the first of the year, so we decided we'd spend one more holiday there before we say goodbye. It's more sentimental for John and Dina of course."

"Truly?" She signaled for the waitress to bring some coffee. "Why, then, that tone of sadness?"

He shrugged. "Still some of the old regrets I suppose. Remember I told you that forgiving dad required me to acknowledge the good memories we'd shared." She nodded. "Lana and Dina have been talking about different reflections, and I have to admit there's more to process than I thought there would be. And then..."

The waitress interrupted with the coffee. After she left, Tommy hesitated to continue his line of thought.

"'And then,'" Sherry urged.

"And then… there's a box." She looked at him askance, and he took the next moments describing the container, how it'd come to him, and Lana's question about what specifically he'd like to find therein, and his fear of doing so.

"Hmm. That's a good question. Mine would be different however."

"Oh really, what for instance?" He folded his hands together on the table and leaned forward.

"I'd have to begin with why? Why do you want to know whatever it is that you're searching for?"

He slumped backward. "I'm not following you, Sherry."

"Okay, I'll slow down. What do want to know? What's your driving purpose?"

"I thought it would be nice to know why Dad was the way he was that's all. What made him so unloving, cold—indifferent? I believe I sincerely forgave him. But I still feel…I don't know. Maybe if I knew why he was who he was, it wouldn't hurt."

"Maybe you're confusing the pain of forgiveness with the purpose of it." She waved at a departing customer then grasped her cup with both hands and sipped while he pondered what she'd said. After a moment, he shrugged and she continued.

"A lot of people don't appreciate the difference between the pain of forgiveness and the purpose of forgiveness. And because they don't understand the distinction, they still feel hurt when they dwell on the person or situation, and they think they haven't forgiven. But forgiveness is the absence of malice, not the absence of pain. Forgiveness is a decision not to strike back, despite the pain."

"Seems like I've heard that somewhere before."

"I'm sure you have," Sherry replied. "It's certainly not original with me, but I've found it to be very true."

"Regarding your mom you mean?"

"And others. But do you think that's a fair assessment of what you're feeling?" She set down her cup and looked him in the eye.

"To be honest I'm not sure I fully understand your point."

"Okay...how's this? Maybe you're afraid to look in the box because you think it means you haven't forgiven your father. To search for answers as to what happened between you and your dad doesn't mean you didn't forgive. Maybe you'll find deeper healing if you look for some answers. Does that sound reasonable?"

"Well...yes...uh...I mean, maybe."

Sherry threw her head back and laughed. "Now there is a statement of confidence. When do you plan to examine the letters and documents in the chest?"

"John and Sally are due in this afternoon."

He glanced down at his watch. "In fact they might be there now. We may get a chance to begin the exploration this evening. And I'm as nervous as a cat! You know me, always getting my hopes up over nothing. I'm afraid I'll expect too much and wind up disappointed. I wouldn't know where to begin looking for answers if there's nothing in the box. All Dad's close relatives are dead, and I can't imagine being comfortable talking to the few friends that might still be living." He shook his head. "I'd have no idea where to start."

"Though you feel a desperate need to try, right?" Tommy nodded. Sherry took his hand for a moment. "I understand. Let's keep it simple and go back to Lana's suggestion. If you narrow the search to one thing, there's less chance of a letdown. So, if there was, if you could name just one thing you'd like to know about your dad, what would it be?"

Tommy placed his hand on his chin and closed his eyes. One thought came suddenly, something he'd never considered before. But that was silly, childish, he wouldn't ask for that. He heard the waitress draw near and stop to refill his coffee and though he tried to ignore the words exchanged by her and Sherry, a single word from their brief dialogue penetrated his consciousness—fishing. Tommy felt his spirit sag, his eyes moistened, and he hesitated to open them knowing Sherry would note the change.

But he couldn't sit like this for the rest of the afternoon. He forced the lids open.

"Th-there is one thing. Yes…if I could only learn one thing…that would be it."

"Which is?" Sherry leaned forward expectantly.

"Uh… it's a story I never told anyone, not even Lana, until last year. About a promise Dad made to me the day before a fishing trip when I was young. He failed to keep that vow, and it's always bothered me. He struck me then as sincere, so determined to change the direction of our relationship—and just like that"—Tommy snapped his fingers—"he went back to his old self without any explanation or apology. If there was only one thing? Yeah, that would do. The one question I'd really like answered if it were possible; why he didn't keep that promise."

Sherry leaned back when he was done, a sad look on her face. Then her lips curled up into a wry smile.

"Maybe you're right. Perhaps you shouldn't get your hopes up." They both chuckled, and the conversation shifted to other events that had occurred in the past year. Sherry was very serious for a moment as she described the stress of being a small business owner when suddenly she looked up, and a broad, pleasing smile filled her face. Tommy turned to see what had brought about this change and saw a stocky fellow with sandy blond hair and abundant freckles approaching the table with a smile as large as Sherry's. When he reached the booth, he leaned over and planted a kiss on her cheek.

"Tommy," Sherry began through her beaming expression. "This is Dexter Evans. Dex is my fiancée."

"Wow!" Tommy exclaimed, grasping Dex's outstretched hand. "This really has been a great year for you; Congratulations to you both. When were you going to tell me?"

Sherry giggled. "I knew Dexter was coming in soon, so I decided to wait until he got here to spring the news on you." She then flowed into the details of how and when they'd met, when he'd popped the question, and the date for the wedding almost without breathing. Tommy couldn't resist smiling. He was thrilled that love and happiness had returned to this lifelong friend.

"I hope you and Lana will be able to come to the wedding," Sherry said looking at Dexter.

"Of course we'll come. I can't wait to tell Lana. She'll be as thrilled as I. Which reminds me," Tommy said glancing at his watch. "I need to run now. I've got to pick up a few things at the convenience mart and then get back up the hill to greet my brother John and his wife Sally."

Tommy shook Dexter's hand again and gave Sherry a hug as she stood. "It was nice to meet you Dex. Hope to see you again before we… Hey! Why don't you guys come to dinner one day this week?"

"Can you squeeze us in with the holiday," Dexter asked.

"Absolutely. No problem at all. Lana will be delighted I assure you. The only night which is taken is Christmas Eve, so that gives us four nights. How about Friday?"

The happy couple looked at each other, shared notes, and then agreed for Friday at six.

"You remember how to get there, don't you Sherry?"

"I could never forget that," she replied as she cuddled up next to Dexter.

"I'll see you Friday evening then, if not before. Good-bye!"

Chapter Eight

It was seven fifteen when Tommy pushed away from the dinner table. The meal had been stupendous, the conversation lively, filled with laughter and memories, a welcome contrast to the strain of last year's gathering. The reunion was bittersweet at times for Tommy, especially when John and Dina shared their memories. Tommy found himself envious of the father they'd known, making him all the more anxious to get to the letters. What a conflict of emotions he was feeling. Almost desperate to see if there were any answers in the documents inside the box—yet fearful that the quest would prove fruitless, perhaps hurtful. Was there something there he might not wish to find? Perhaps some things were better left unsaid, unknown. Yet he couldn't shake the growing feeling that there was a reason the box had come to him.

"So this is the mysterious container." John had risen from the table and walked over to where the carved coffer had lain neglected since last evening. "Very pretty. You say Richard Dorian dropped it off."

Tommy nodded vigorously. "Yes. Do you remember him?"

"No... well, yes but only vaguely. I doubt I'd recognize him on the street." John grabbed the box and laid it in the middle of coffee table, then pulled the table closer to the couch and sat down. "No time like the present to see what secrets are contained therein. Any objections?"

Tommy gulped. "None... that I can think of." He pulled a chair up across from John. Dina nodded her agreement and slid forward on the couch as Wayne and Lana looked on. John turned the latch and raised the lid revealing the clutter of papers, envelopes, and a smattering of photos.

Dina grabbed the picture she'd seen yesterday evening. "John, do you know where this was taken? It seems familiar to me, but like Tommy, I can't place it."

John studied the 3 x 5 for a moment then shrugged. "I'm afraid not. It doesn't look familiar to me at all. Boy they were young then, weren't they?"

They nodded their agreement and continued through the dozen or so pictures. Most were scenes of the house at different times of the year. Tommy was studying the photo of the parents which Dina thought so familiar when John interrupted his thoughts.

"Wait a minute... what's this?" He held up a weathered picture of some men standing before a boat and a large body of water with a young man in front. "Tommy is this you?"

Tommy took the photo from his brother's hand as the others looked on. He gave it a casual glance but then... he drew it close to his face. Lana must've seen his forehead grow tight for she leaned in to look closer.

"Tommy... what is it honey?"

"It's...uh...it's a fishing trip—*the* fishing trip—the one I told you about." He remembered his conversation with Sherry as goose pimples ran along his spine. "When... uh...when Dad made his promise."

She stood upright gasping as Tommy turned to her and their eyes met. He'd told her of his conversation with Sherry before dinner and what he'd said he wished to learn.

"What trip? What promise?" Dina and John asked in unison, their eyes pleading for insight. He'd never told them about the episode with his dad at the overlook, the day of the promise, the day before those gathered in the photo were captured on film.

He understood his siblings' natural confusion. He'd kept so much from them through the years. What mystified him was how unnatural he suddenly felt. Odd that he still didn't feel comfortable giving them all the details of the conversation he'd had with his father that day so long ago. Why should he feel such a drive to keep secrets from them now? He had little time to ponder and could only bring himself to remind them of the yearly trip their father took and of Tommy accompanying him that particular year.

"Gee that's odd." John retrieved the photo and scrutinized it. "I wonder what he felt was so important about this particular trip that he would save the picture from that year."

"Perhaps the fact that Tommy was with him," Lana offered while gazing deeply into her husband's eyes.

Tommy gulped. *Could there be an answer here after all?*

They passed the photo to Dina, then Wayne, everyone agreeing the young man was indeed Tommy, before returning it to him. He took it and was about to lay it on the stack with the others. But as he glanced at it again something caught his eye. It was impossible to hide his reaction.

"What is it Tommy?" Sally leaned in across his shoulder. A long, breathless silence drew the others attention also.

"Oh... uh... nothing much. I was just struck by the odd clothes I was wearing, that's all. I never was in style as a child."

The answer seemed to satisfy the others, and they moved on, but Tommy felt Lana's gaze and as he turned he perceived a wondering, pensive expression.

There were about three hundred envelopes and documents stuffed tightly in the small container. It would certainly take more than this hour or two to sort through them all, so John suggested they proceed with the newest looking of the documents. They were trivial legal matters about the land, house, tax papers, but much to Tommy's angst, no helpful revelations about his father. He wrung his hands while the others wrangled over what to do with particular selections. Save this? Trash that?

"I can't imagine why Dad would keep this." John sighed after another half hour. "Or, why he would have left Tommy an engraved box, unless he wanted you to have this picture." He lifted the photo and handed it to his brother. "So in case that was his thought, Tommy, you better take this and put it among your things, so you don't lose it."

Tommy took it and stuffed it into his shirt pocket for the time being. "I think it's going to get a bit cool tonight," he said pushing away from the table. "I'm going to get an armload of wood for the night. Lana how about some hot cocoa and cookies?"

The children wandering into the great room just then cheered as Sally and Lana went off to the kitchen. Dina slid back into the couch and Wayne's embrace as John closed the lid of the box. Tommy went out to the porch for wood and lingered there in the cold darkness, his mind jumbled with thoughts and prayers. He pushed them aside and returned before the others became suspicious.

The family nibbled at Christmas cookies for a time, sipping hot cocoa and eggnog, talking about life, and growing sleepy. Around ten, the children were in their respective rooms their chatter slowly dying as John and Sally bade them goodnight. Wayne and Dina slid off to their room, and Lana kissed her husband who was sitting by the fire, gazing down on the lights of Destiny. After everyone was gone, left only with the crackling of the fire, Tommy pulled the photo out of his pocket—and wondered.

Chapter Nine

The next morning started as the previous had, with a determined and persistent Maggie gleefully animated over the frost. One thing was different. Tommy had already risen. His sleep had been fitful, up and down twenty times, each rising a battle to silence his turbulent thoughts. Exploring the letters was meant to bring him peace, tranquility, answers. He found more questions instead. *Why did Dad keep an obscure picture from a distant and, for all I know, meaningless time? Am I meant to learn something from it?*

Maggie's entrance however caused him to push all these things aside. He worked at stoking the fire, then fixed her some breakfast. After pouring another cup of coffee, he sat next to the window watching the sun reflect off the frost as it climbed higher above the eastern horizon. Soon Lana joined him. Typical morning small talk dominated the conversation until it turned back to the letters. Lana stood warming herself by the stove, hands clasped around a cup of cocoa.

"Will you tell me what you wouldn't tell Sally last night?"

"I didn't think I could fool you." Tommy looked up with a smile. "I can't be sure, so I'm hesitant to say."

"Certain about what?" she persisted.

He rose from his chair and walked over to her while pulling the photo from his pocket. "You see that man right there," he said pointing to a person behind the others in the group.

"Yes, I see him. But it's hard to make out his features," she replied while squinting at the image. "Who is it?"

"I can't be sure, and forgive the obvious conspiracy theory connotations, but it looks very much like Richard Dorian."

"Dorian? The gentleman who brought you the box in the first place?"

Tommy nodded, returning the photo to his pocket then falling into the couch. "Yes. At least it looks like him. Much younger of course, but there's definitely a resemblance. It might be just my imagination. You know, wanting to see more than there is. On the other hand, I did have that feeling that we'd met before. It might be because I'd seen him before."

She walked over and sat beside him. "That's possible. But it would be a rather strange coincidence if it were him, wouldn't it?"

"Eerily so. The problem is I have no way of knowing whether it's him or not, nor any way of finding out. Remember he left no card, no address, nothing!" Even he heard the exasperation rising in his voice.

Lana took his hand and kissed it. "Don't fret over it. Maybe you'll find something today that will clarify things further. You are planning to study the letters some more, yes?"

"It's not possible until after lunch, unless I do so alone. Wayne and Dina have some shopping to do this morning, while John has an appointment with a realtor this afternoon. I've promised the boys we'd take a hike sometime this week. Today would be as good a day as any. I guess this evening will be the earliest."

The boys were murmuring around the breakfast table by this time and yelled hooray approvingly at his announced intention. Tommy and Lana looked at each other smiling and went to join the others, all of them up now and milling about in the kitchen. The hustle and bustle of the next hour distressed Tommy, first because he couldn't keep his focus off the questions the photo had generated. Yet he was also dismayed that so much of their time this week was to be spent like any other week of the year, where schedules crowded in and demanded attention. Where would they find time for Christmas when their days seemed so terribly normal and commonplace? This would be the last holiday he observed in this house and with his passion for Christmas, the celebration was sacred to him,— the bustle and distraction— irreverent. He did his best to stifle the feelings of frustration but they persisted throughout the day despite his effort.

It was around seven that evening before dinner was concluded and they gathered once more to examine the box. Lana and Sally were helping the children string popcorn for a garland to decorate the tree, and softly singing carols. John was sipping on hazelnut scented coffee, watching his siblings indifferently from a chair by the stove while Tommy and Dina situated the container before them. Tommy was doing his best not to let on how desperate he wanted to explore the contents.

"Look." Dina pulled a large manila envelope from the bottom of the box, sending a flurry of other documents spilling onto the table. "What's this?"

Several other similar envelopes had been pressed together at the bottom causing it to blend in and remain unseen. She pulled the clasp back and removed from it what Tommy guessed to be about thirty or forty yellowed pages of paper. She examined them closely as Tommy shuffled through the sheets on the table.

Lana came over. When she lifted the envelope a circular object slid out onto the table. "Look, a DVD. It's marked, 'Home Movies.'"

"Home movies? This box is full of surprises," Sally exclaimed.

"This is definitely Dad's writing," Dina replied after a few moments of examining the letters.

"Dad's?" John lurched from his seat and came to the table. "I never knew Jesse Howell to write. What do they say?" He carefully took a few pages from the stack of papers and glanced over them with Sally. Tommy was speechless and didn't move, intensely reading the faces of his brother and sister. He shook his head slowly.

No! No, I won't get my hopes up.

Lana took a few pages and flipped through them. "There's no date on these."

"There are no dates on any of them," John returned, glancing at his own handful. His eyes traced down a paragraph or two, he flipped to a new page, and so forth. "I can't make sense of any of this. I can't even make out some of the words."

"No, you wouldn't be able to," Dina replied. "Penmanship was never Dad's strength. But there's no question its Dad's writing. From what I can make out, however, and this seems simply impossible, it sounds like... almost... a journal or diary of some sort."

"A diary?" John and Tommy exclaimed simultaneously as their eyes met. Tommy shook his head and laughed. "No way. No way, Dad kept a diary. A journal? You need to look a little closer sis." Inside, his heart was quivering.

"I'm not saying he consciously *meant* to, but the effect is the same. But since you don't agree, then listen and judge for yourself. *'I saw D again today.'*"

"D? Who is D?" John interrupted.

Tommy's heart sank. He knew who "D" was, and the old tremors of anger stirred a little in his heart.

"It doesn't say," Dina sighed. "It simply has a capitalized letter D." She continued. *'I saw D again today. She asked how I was doing since... I wasn't able to answer. I know what she wants, how she feels. It might be all right, but no. No, I don't think that will happen again.'*"

"See what I mean," Dina stressed. "I'm telling you this is a journal of some sort."

"D...since what? You'd have to be a cryptologist to figure that out," John mumbled returning to his seat and coffee.

Tommy looked at Lana then nodded in response to her questioning eyes. Then she smiled a little and Tommy understood her meaning—there *was* good news in the letters.

"Perhaps Tommy," Lana began, "this would be the right time to tell them who 'D' was."

"Tell us?" John rose from his chair once more.

"You mean you know who this is, Tommy?" Dina pressed.

"Yes…at least, I'm pretty certain. 'D' stands for Denise. Denise Oliver. She was a woman, now deceased, that had been the object of some of Dad's philandering. More specifically… just before Mom died."

"How do you know that?" Dina demanded.

"I learned it from Uncle James, who learned it from Mom, just before she died. She apparently knew what was going on, knew how… much…" The emotional strain was too much on Tommy. He went quiet.

Lana took a deep breath. "She knew how much stress it would cause between Tommy and Jesse if and when he found out. She'd sworn her brother James to silence, a vow he kept until just before he died eight years ago, when he told Tommy that his mother's wish was for him to forgive his father, when he learned the truth."

"So that's why no Christmas at home for seven years," Wayne offered.

"Yes," Tommy nodded. "It took me seven years to find the strength to forgive. Seven wasted years."

The room grew silent for a few minutes except for the laughter and activity of the children in the kitchen. Sally rose and began counting the pages.

"Forty-five; and very fine print on legal size paper at that. If it is a journal, there's quite a bit of material here. Is there anymore in the box?"

"No," Tommy replied. "I just looked. A lot of other documents, and letters but none like those. Are they all the same kind of anonymous observations?"

"Looks like," Dina answered. "Here's another one. *'It happened again last night. That innocent visitor with those hollow, pleading eyes begging me why again and again and... haunting my dreams, keeping me awake— accusing me. I talked it over last week with Dick...'"*

"Dick?" John blurted out.

"That's what it says. Dick." Dina continued. *'I talked it over last week with Dick, and he gave me the same reminders as before. Try as I might it just hasn't helped. Dear God how long must this phantom abide my dreams?'"*

Dina and John both looked at Tommy who shrugged. "Sorry, no idea this time."

Dina dropped the letter on the stack of others, put her hands on her hips and leaned upright in her chair. "My back is killing me." She moaned. Wayne began rubbing her shoulders.

John grabbed a sugar cookie from the platter before him. "If you have time and the desire to read all forty-five pages you might make sense of them. But I don't see any value in that. It was nice of Mr. Dorian to drop them off, but I think we'll find them useless for the most part." He pushed away from the table, went into the great room, and clicked on the TV. "Christmas movie time," he yelled out, which brought the children running to find the best seats, Maggie with ornaments still in hand.

Sally gathered the letters together, slid them into an envelope and tossed it back into the box. Tommy and Lana found a seat near the stove, and the family shared a joyful holiday favorite. Bodily, Tommy was in the room with the rest of them, but mentally he was in that box, wondering whether he'd find proof there of his father's love. He couldn't wait till morning when the house was quiet, and he could take a look at them for himself.

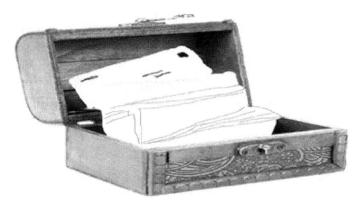

Chapter Ten

Tommy crept quietly down the hall around five-thirty the next morning. A dim orange glow from the fire guided him through the darkness. Reaching the stove, he threw in a few pieces of wood. In the kitchen, he clicked on the coffee, grabbed a blueberry muffin, and took a seat with his coffee near the fire, the manila envelope full of letters in his lap. He picked one at random and began reading.

"Can't make out that first word," he murmured. "Oh well."

....missed school again today. Been missing a lot lately. I'm sickened by this, yet what can I do? I can't undo what happened. It's unfair, terribly unfair. His beef is with me, or should be,

not with him. But he's the one who'll have to stand up. It's his decision. Maybe if she was here...

Tommy read the paragraph twice then lay the page aside, took another gulp of coffee, and tore off more of the muffin. He stared at the ceiling for a moment, his mind chewing over the possible implications as forcefully as he chewed the morsel in his mouth. He shook his head.

"This might be harder than I thought," he muttered. "If there were names or dates, I could make some sense of this. With all these 'he's, and 'she's,' Dad might be talking about anybody."

A shuffle startled him, and he turned around. There was Dina, hands on her lower back.

"Are you talking to yourself?" she whispered.

He snickered and shook his head. "Not at all. I heard you coming."

"You did not, liar. I saw you jump." She giggled and slid onto the couch. "I'll be so glad when this baby gets here. I couldn't lay in that bed another minute. Not what I'm used to at home. That's my excuse. What are you doing up at this time of the morning?"

He flourished the letters before her. "Trying to make sense of these."

"I see. Any luck?"

"Not so far. I just got started." He winked at her. "And since you heard me, you know my complaint. No names, no dates."

"You sound disappointed. This means a lot to you?"

"Honestly? Yes. More than I thought, frankly. I've tried not getting my hopes up about the possibility. Looks like I've failed—again. Would you like some coffee?"

"Please with the same instructions as before." Dina squirmed around trying to get comfortable as Tommy saluted and went to the kitchen his cup in hand.

"Let me see that one, yes the one you were just reading," she requested as Tommy returned. He passed the sheet of paper over, and she read the section aloud. "Let's use some logic here. Even though it isn't dated, we can make some inferences that might help us understand."

"Such as?"

"Well, for example, this phrase, 'Maybe if *she* was here...' I'd have to think *she* means mom, so the letter would've been written after Mom died."

Tommy nodded through another bite of the muffin. "Sounds fair. But when after Mom died?"

"I'd say soon after. Dad wasn't the type to mourn for years you know, at least not to us, although these letters might give us other insights."

"What makes you think they could?"

"The letter last night, of course. Didn't you notice the tone of resignation, regret about his relationship with Denise?"

"Oh yeah." Tommy snarled. He instantly regretted the tone. "Sorry Dina. I held on to my grudge against Denise for seven years. Old habits are hard to break. I believe I've forgiven Dad, still he did have other romantic interests you might remember. *She* might be one of them."

"Possibly." Dina nodded, stealing a portion of his muffin. "Yet in fairness we can't condemn the relationships he had after Mom died, right? So then, we look at the other clues. Wasn't there a period not long after Mom died that you missed a lot of school?"

Tommy paused, leaned back in his chair, head cocked to the side for a moment. "Let me see that," he snatched the paper back from her hand and re-read the last two lines aloud.

"Is it possible? 'His beef is with me, or should be.'" He stared at the letter.

"What does it mean?" Dina pressed. He held up his index finger requesting a moment more for reflection. She crossed her arms and waited. "Tommy?"

"Do you recall…? I was in the ninth grade. This guy who'd just gotten out of reform school for murder was bullying me. I was terrified. And he told me… the reason he'd singled me out was because Dad had made him leave a Ruritan club dance… for uh, misbehaving somehow. He wanted me to pay back the money he lost because he was ejected. Do you remember?"

Dina shook her head. "No, I don't. I just remember you missing a lot of school. Was that why?"

"That was about a year after Mom died. Just about a year later…" He pulled the page close and read it aloud again, emphasizing the words. "'His beef… should be with me.' That must be what he's talking about…"

The possibility gave rise to a torrent of emotions he couldn't fully control. That threat—those times were some of the darkest in his teen years. He'd felt alone, with no one to talk it over with, nowhere to turn for answers. A horrible loneliness worsened by belief his father hadn't cared about his pain.

If this letter is taking about that time—Dad did care, and very much.

He wanted to trust these words were about him, grasped for the joy they might bring. But the recollection struck a sad tone as well. Tommy reflected back on how he'd blamed his dad for the problem. Like another time when he'd suffered for his father's decisions.

His dad, acting as umpire in a softball game, had called a young man out on a close play at home. Later in a dark corner of the facility the young man knocked Tommy down, and stuffed grass in his mouth as punishment. How helpless Tommy had felt, what anger!

And the second time? The day he walked carelessly out of Science Class only to be grabbed roughly and thrown against the wall of lockers by a face he'd never seen. Attacked again for what his father had done. Had the first event affected his perception of the latter? Yes, he'd blamed his dad, not only for the confrontation, but for his perceived apathy as well. And yet why? He'd never mentioned the first incident to his father.

He could see it all now. His own prideful stubbornness had been the reason his father couldn't help him. It wasn't fatherly indifference at all, it was a high wall built by a bitter, unforgiving son. But if that were true then—

Tommy grabbed the letters and began poring over them, searching with new enthusiasm for further sections that might refer to him. Easier said than done. His father's writing was often illegible, the forty-five or so pages written in very small print. Still, Tommy came to another section after a few moments that seemed promising.

I broke my promise. I swore to myself I wouldn't do that. I know I'll be blamed... at some point. I found out the truth... on the trip. I'm sorry. That hurt... still hurts... too much. That's the only excuse I have. Awful of me to say that after all the pain I caused her. Besides, how could I have told him? How do you tell that?

Tommy sighed, and buried his face in his hands.

"What's wrong, Tommy?" Dina laid her hand on his shoulder. "What did that one say?"

"I can't make out what it *means*, Dina. I can read this—but I can't understand. Listen." He reread the section to her. "What promise is he talking about? What truth did he learn that made him break it? What could possibly have hurt him that much? Who is the 'him' he couldn't tell?"

"That's the most important question isn't it?"

Tommy looked at his sister's faint smile. He saw what she was hinting at, knew the answer. He needed to hear her say the words. "What do you mean?"

"Are these letters speaking about you? That's what you're after isn't it?"

He nodded, pushing away from the table, lifting his coffee cup. "Like some more?"

Dina stood, waddled over to the picture window and drew back the shades. "Not just yet, thanks."

Tommy returned in a moment, sipping on the hot liquid, and stood next to her, gazing out at the brightening eastern sky. A moment or two passed in silence. Would he ever find the answers he sought in this jumble of letters? He sighed, his chin slumped against his chest. He filled his lungs, and turned to his sister.

"How can I possibly tell whether any of those writings are about me, or for me? Am I setting myself up for disappointment? Tell me the truth."

Dina shook her head. "I don't know what

the truth is. I'm certain those letters were written by Dad, one of the events at least has an eerie coincidence to your life. The box has an engraving addressed to Tommy. Beyond that, neither of us knows very much. If you really want to learn, you'll have to pour over them, examine every detail that seems to speak about you, or to you. Unless you can find someone who has some further info or insight into Dad's private life, you'll have to take it on faith that Dad was talking about you. I see no other way to answer your question."

She smiled at her brother, gave him a gentle hug, then wobbled back to the bedroom. Something she'd just said was reverberating through Tommy's mind— *unless you can find someone who has further insight into Dad's private life*. Tommy wandered toward the stove. The fire was roaring, the wood popping and cracking, the metal pinging away with the heat. He placed his cup on the stove, holding his hands up to further warm them. Abruptly he clapped them together.

Of course. Yes, that could work.

He dashed off to the bedroom, returning in a moment with the photo of the fishing trip in his hand. He scrutinized the portion with the person resembling Richard Dorian, twisting to view it from different angles before letting his hand drop to his side. Retrieving his coffee cup, he noticed a pen and pad of paper lying on the antique desk.

He rushed over, plopped down in the chair, and began making notes about his observations.

He scribbled a number of ideas over the next hour, interrupted by coffee trips or attention to the fire. Near eight o'clock Lana shuffled down the hall.

"Good morning." She rubbed her eyes, yawning. "What time did you get up?"

"Way before the sun did." He chuckled. "How'd you sleep?"

"Fine." She looked about the room and leaned into the kitchen. "Where's Magpie?"

"Believe it or not, she's still in bed."

"In bed?" Lana blurted out. "What got you up so early?"

Tommy held the letters in his hand.

"I should have known." She smiled, went and poured a cup of coffee, then pulled a chair up next to him. "So, did you find anything?"

"Maybe; look at this picture. Remember I told you that this person here looks like Mr. Dorian?" She nodded. "How old do you think he looks there?"

"I can't tell honey. It's not very clear."

"Give me your best guess."

She took the photo from his hand and subjected it to the same examination he'd conducted earlier. "Maybe forty-five."

"That's my estimate also, though I've never been good at age guessing."

She sipped her coffee as he looked at the

photo. "So what does that mean?"

"That the person in this photo could not have been the man who brought me the box. If we're right about the age of the man in the picture, he'd be close to seventy today. The Richard Dorian I met couldn't have been more than fifty." He tossed the picture down.

"Why is that important?" Lana asked.

"Dina and I were talking earlier. The only way to find out whether the things in these letters have anything to do with me, with why Dad was the way he was, is to talk to someone who knew him, someone who'd have known him back then. I've been sitting here thinking, and all the others in that photo are deceased I'm sure."

Lana picked up the picture pointing at the mystery person. "You think he might still be alive?"

"Maybe. It's possible."

"But you said he was too old to be the person who brought you the box. How can you be sure this person's name is Dorian?"

"The resemblance is uncanny, too close to be a coincidence. At least it seems so from this." He stood, waving the photo as he did. "I'm going into town to have the photo enlarged. That should help settle that question. I'm going to the courthouse and the library to see if any Dorians lived near here. Is that all right with you?"

She hugged Tommy then looked up into his face. "Of course, try not to be out too long. You need to spend more Christmas time with the children."

"I'll just be a couple of hours. See you later." He planted a soft kiss on her forehead, and half an hour later he was gone.

Chapter Eleven

Just after one o'clock, Tommy pulled into the drive to find his three children sitting sullen and inactive on the porch. Lana came out the door also looking somewhat frustrated. Maggie brightened a little at his return, walking out to meet him at the van.

"Well, what's the problem around here?" He lifted Maggie as he greeted the boys.

"I'll tell you what's wrong," Lana began. "Our children are used to living in the hustle of Charleston, a large southern city. They're unaccustomed to country solitude, and bored out of their minds. John and Sally took their children shopping for a few more gifts leaving these three to entertain each other." Lana crossed her arms. Tommy recognized a pleading glimmer in her eye.

"So now that you understand why we all have a little cabin fever, any suggestions to remedy this restlessness?" Lana nodded toward the children as they looked on. Tommy glanced at his watch, then at the lowering sun.

"We've time for another short hike along the ridge if you'd like that." The words were barely out of his mouth when a cheer went up. Danny and T.J. leapt from the porch, barreling for the woods.

"Whoa, hold on boys," Tommy interrupted. "Although it's a great afternoon, you'll need your jackets in a little while. Run and get them. You too, Magpie." The three scurried off while Tommy threw some bottles of water plus energy bars into a knapsack, grabbed his own jacket, then taking Lana by the hand, led the five onto the path that disappeared into the pines.

They plodded along the trail Tommy had selected, winding gradually upwards for about half a mile. Maggie complained whenever the boys failed to wait for her, prompting Tommy's fatherly reminder that this was meant to be fun for them all.

"Okay," they moaned, crossing their arms and tapping their feet impatiently till Maggie caught up.

They hiked for almost an hour before the

pine-dotted rocky crags opened up into a spacious mountaintop meadow. Some whitetail deer were grazing a couple hundred yards in the distance prompting a joyful glee from Maggie. This sent them dashing away, much to the boys' dismay. Destiny lay visible in the valley below. Tommy and Lana looked for a seat.

"Come up here, Lana." Tommy extended his hand and pulled his wife up a steep incline next to a rock outcropping, on which they sat down. Pulling the knapsack around into his lap he opened the zipper. "Something to drink?"

"Yes, thank you. That made me very thirsty. Hey kids," Lana called out. "Come get a drink and snack before you go too far."

The children dashed to the bottom of the incline where Tommy dropped down a bottle of water and energy bar for them to share. They sat quietly for a moment, taking in the brisk invigorating mountain air.

"See that house?" Tommy pointed to a tiny speck about two miles distant. "The yellow one there."

Lana took another gulp of water. "Yes I do. Whose house is that?"

"That's where Sherry lived and grew up." Tommy rocked his dangling feet over the rock's edge. "Dad's house is just behind that clump of trees. I haven't been here for years."

"Really?" Lana exclaimed. "You seemed to be quite familiar with the route despite that."

Tommy looked out over the valley. "This used to be one of my favorite getaway spots when I was a boy, especially when Dad and I had one of our clashes. I'd come up here to remind myself that the world was bigger than my problems. Always helped me clear my head, to refocus."

She took his hand in hers. "Is that why you chose this destination today?"

He looked into her eyes, nodding. "I guess so. Got you and the children out of the house for a while anyway. And a good stretch of the legs for all of us."

"Yes, thank God. I was running out of ideas for keeping the kids busy. You don't realize how many diversions there are at home to keep them occupied until you're away from home. I'm very thankful we were able to share this together. Back to my original question. Why this place? I assume your investigation was unfruitful."

"Pretty much, I hate to admit. The photo enlargement didn't help... at least it didn't seem so to me. I'll get your opinion when we get back to the house."

"And the other? The Dorians?"

"Not a Dorian in the county. I even stopped in at Sherry's Plate, asked some of the old timers in there. No one ever heard of a Dorian family around here. Another strikeout."

"Brrrr." Lana pulled her jacket close. Tommy put his arm around her and drew her near. "Cools down quick up here, doesn't it?"

"Yes—but think about how good the fire will feel when we get back. Though we'll only be able to stay a few more minutes," Tommy offered, "I'll make sure the kids wear themselves out good by the time they get home."

"I'm all for that as long as you don't make it too hard on me."

"Hey, you three," Tommy called out and waved. "We need to head back." The trio began trekking toward their parents as Tommy pointed out some other landmarks visible in the valley below.

"So what are you going to do," Lana asked a few minutes later as they climbed down from their perch. A cold December wind swept across the ridge, prompting Tommy to shield her with his body.

"I'm not sure what I can do. I have no way to contact Richard Dorian if he's even connected to my so-called quest. There are no Dorians in this area to ask, the picture is inconclusive. I suppose I'll just have to be satisfied with searching through the documents and letters in that box to see what else I can learn."

As they started back down the trail, the children rejoined them. "What next? If you can't find anything?"

"I'll have to do as Dina suggests and take what I do find on faith. I'll set the matter aside and concentrate on giving my family a great Christmas."

Lana smiled, yet he knew his words hadn't convinced her. He wasn't very good at setting things aside, especially something like this.

**

The evening back at the house was filled with holiday busyness. With only four more days till Christmas, they'd agreed to spend this night decorating. John picked up a cedar on the way home, then he, and Wayne erected the tree in its usual location in the great room. Dinner consisted of sandwiches accompanied by soup plus an abundance of Christmas snacks and delicacies. Slices of baked ham, stuffing balls, summer sausage, and cheese, candy canes and Hershey's Kisses, disappeared throughout the evening.

Dina directed the action from the most comfortable spot on the couch. The children were forever getting in each other's way either from a desire to help decorate or to start putting gifts beneath the tree. They chattered non-stop, predicting who was getting what. Tommy and Lana made sure the fire was roaring, the cocoa abundant. Sally, a tremendous singer, serenaded them throughout the evening with carols.

Finally, about eight-thirty, with the task completed, the family gathered around the great room and the lights were extinguished.

"Everyone ready?" Wayne called out.

"Yes, yes!" The children cried in unison. The switch was flipped, the air was filled with "oohs" and "aahs," that added to the magic of the twinkling colorful glow, followed by a stampede of kids bearing gifts to be stacked beneath the holiday icon. Pandemonium reigned for another twenty minutes till the children began to wind down. An hour later only Tommy and John remained. Tommy placed the box on the table again to renew his search.

John slid into a chair next to him. "I think we should have copies of these photos made for each of us," he offered.

"That's a good idea." Tommy gathered up the pictures and nodded. "Too bad I didn't get this sooner. They'd have made great Christmas gifts from us to you guys."

John nodded his agreement, then flipped through a few papers. "Find anything helpful?"

Tommy breathed deeply then shook his head. "I'm afraid not. A few snippets of information here and there, which may or may not refer to me. Certainly not enough yet for me to accept the fact that Dad meant for me to have the box."

"You still think it's possible the engraving is a coincidence?" John looked at his brother with what Tommy took as a gleam of pity.

"Yes," Tommy replied softly. "Yes I do."

John picked up the enlarged fishing picture. "This didn't help."

"No. I did that in the hopes of getting more detail of the man, right there." Tommy placed his finger next to the man. "It didn't help."

"And who is that?" John scrutinized the picture.

"I'm not sure. He looks very much like the Richard Dorian who brought me the box."

"Oh, I see." John's eyebrows lifted. "You thought if it were, he could help you somehow."

"Yes that's right."

John laid the photo down. "So what's the problem?"

"In the first place that man is too old to be 'my' Mr. Dorian. In the second, there are no Dorians around here to ask." Tommy lifted the original photo and shook his head again. "Looks like I'm at an impasse."

"Maybe not."

"What do you mean?"

"Well, perhaps you're going about this the wrong way," John suggested.

"I'm not following you."

"You're looking for Dorians around here right?" Tommy nodded. "Maybe you should be looking for them somewhere else." Tommy slid back in his chair, uncertain what his brother's point was.

"Where was this picture taken?"

"Over near... Edenton, on the Albemarle Sound." Tommy snapped his fingers. "Of course, why didn't I think of that?" He leapt from his chair, grabbed the phone from his jacket pocket, and dialed long-distance information. A few moments later he'd scribbled five-phone numbers on a scratch pad. He glanced up at the clock. Ten forty-five.

"Too late to call tonight," John offered.

"You're right. I'll have to wait till morning. Still, thanks to you I may have a few more options." Tommy smiled then patted his brother's back.

John stood sliding his chair under the table with a grin. "You're welcome. Now, I'm off to bed. See you in the morning."

Pages in hand, Tommy grunted as his brother disappeared down the hall. Sleep had disappeared from his eyes, and he dove anew into Jesse's Journal.

Chapter Twelve

The clock read nine-fifteen as Tommy pulled himself from bed the next morning. He'd been up past three searching through the letters, copying the pertinent sections onto a legal pad to make sorting them easier. He was so beat from the effort and emotions of the endeavor even Maggie couldn't keep him awake.

She'd rushed in a little before seven, exuberant once more about the possibility of a white Christmas. A cold front was pushing through the region with some snow squalls and showers but no expected accumulation. He fell back asleep after Lana rose and led her out of the room. By the time Tommy staggered bleary-eyed into the kitchen, Maggie's joy was gone. She sat sulking by the window.

"Good morning," Lana called as he stumbled in.

"Hey, babe. I need an eye opener." He rubbed his eyes, brushing back the black locks of hair hanging in them.

She stood, pulled a cup from the cabinet and poured the last of the previous pot of coffee into it. "This has been warming for a while, so it should be good and strong. I'll make a fresh pot now."

"Thanks." He took the mug from her hand. "I'm going to need more."

"What time did you come to bed anyhow?" Lana placed a platter of fruit and donuts before him. "I looked at the clock about one, you still weren't there."

"After three. I just couldn't tear myself away from the letters." He turned up the goblet for the last drop of coffee just as the beeper went off signaling the fresh supply was ready. "More, please."

"Where in the world did you get all the energy?" She poured another serving as he devoured an orange wedge. "After the hike and the decorating, I was beat. Didn't you say something about setting the letters aside if you couldn't find anything helpful?"

He stretched, yawning, before popping a couple of grapes in his mouth. "I did say that, and I meant it, really I did."

She laughed. "So what happened to change your mind?"

"John pointed something out to me I'd missed altogether."

"Which was?"

"I was looking for the Dorians around here. John hinted that since the picture was taken near Edenton, perhaps the Dorians were near there also. I got five numbers last night to call today, though none of them were of a Richard Dorian. That little bit of daylight renewed my enthusiasm, I just couldn't tear myself away. I didn't go to sleep for another thirty minutes even after I came to bed I was so pumped up." He grabbed a muffin and with a nod for her to follow, headed for a chair by the stove. "Where is everyone?"

"Sally got a call from one of her relatives to come visit, so they'll be gone past lunch. The parents-to-be went to town for breakfast, they said. I think they just wanted some alone time. She also mentioned they were going to swing by your father's grave before they come back. The boys are out exploring. Magpie is sulking. She didn't like my insistence that these snow squalls wouldn't amount to anything. That girl has your stubborn streak!"

Tommy giggled. "Yes, I'm afraid she does."

"So?" Lana motioned toward the letters. "What did you find that was so energizing, besides the Dorian info I mean."

"See for yourself." He handed her the legal pad of notes. "I still can't make much out of them, yet all I've written there I'm sure refers to me. Read... uh, the one I-I circled... at the top."

Lana moved up the page with her finger until she reached the designated section, reading aloud. "'I took some books to the hospital tonight. It was hard to do, very hard. Tried to talk to the boy … couldn't find the words. She was there again as always, lurking in the shadows of the room. The effort was too painful, I left the comics. Forgive me son.'"

Lana looked up just as Tommy wiped his eye. "Honey? What's wrong?" she asked. "This *is* about you then?"

He nodded, still unable to speak for a moment. He swallowed hard and cleared his throat.

"Mostly anyway. That...w-was... the uh, story I tol-told you once about when I was in the hospital with a kidney injury… do you recall me telling you about that?"

"Yes, I remember."

"Well…. I'm confused about the 'she' he referenced since Mom was gone by then. The rest is definitely about me."

"One more proof your father did care about you—much more than you knew."

"Uh-huh." Tommy pulled out a handkerchief and wiped his nose. "These letters still don't explain why he never just told me he cared."

"I… don't know. Perhaps there's some hint in 'she.' You don't think that refers to your mom?"

"I don't see how. She'd died before that."

"Okay… maybe he meant it figuratively, like guilt association. He was so ashamed of the way he treated her that I…I'm just guessing."

"And doing a fine job except for this line about 'lurking in the shadows.' Plus, what about this?" He pointed to the word *she* circled at the top of his notes.

"What's that?"

"Sometimes 'she' or 'her' seems to be a reference to Mom," Tommy continued. "There are other times when those words are clearly speaking of someone else." He flipped the page Lana was holding. "Look at this one for example."

Lana read the words aloud. "'She was so young when it happened. So very young. Could she ever have forgiven me? Can they?' Hmmm... What about the words just above there? 'I saw her last night again.' What can that mean?"

Tommy shoved a piece of wood in the fire. "If you go through them all, the letters I mean, not my notes, you often find those thoughts. I think this was a recurring dream about some trauma involving a young girl."

"How strange." Lana didn't take her eyes from the notes as she spoke.

"I'm hoping to sit down this evening with John and Dina, ask them about the dream. Somehow I don't think they'll know anything either."

Lana laid the pad down then looked into Tommy's eyes. "What would that have to do with his relationship with you?"

He shrugged. "I can't say that it's related. I keep hoping there's a key here in the letters somewhere, but I haven't found one if there is." He clasped his hands at the back of his neck yawning once more. "The two things that keep coming up however are this person in his recurring dream and the resemblance of a man in the photo to Mr. Dorian. If my search for him turns out to be a dead end, I suppose I'll keep the letters as souvenirs, memoirs of Dad. Though I can't imagine why he'd want me, of all people, to have them."

"How do you know the man you want is named Richard?"

"I don't, Lana. Remember in the earlier letter Dad mentioned 'Dick.' That's usually the nickname for Richard. There was no Richard in the phone information, though a couple of the names from information did start with r, so I'm working from that assumption."

"When will you try to call the numbers you found last night?"

Tommy shrugged, walked into the kitchen, poured his third cup of coffee, then returned to the picture window and gazed out for a few moments.

"I'm a little nervous. I think it's one of those 'be careful what you wish for' situations. An innocent expression after Thanksgiving dinner and here comes a box. I've tried very hard not to, but I've gotten my hopes up now, hopes of proof positive that I simply misunderstood Dad all those years. That in spite of all the anger between us he really did love me. I'm afraid I might not find anything, and now that he's gone, if I don't..."

Lana sighed. "One thing's for sure. This is drawing a lot of your emotional energy. You need to get this off your plate before Christmas Day if you can." Lana walked over to snuggle behind him, wrapping her arms around his waist. "To be fair to me and the children."

"I know," he whispered nodding. After emptying the cup, he handed it to her. "I need a wake-up shower."

***

Three hours later Lana found him at the kitchen table, his mood little changed. The scratch pad with the phone numbers he'd found last night lay before him. Lana looked over his shoulder. The lines drawn through the middle of the first four numbers grew in darkness and indentation in the paper. Arrows or circles of doodling framed the page.

"No luck?"

"None. Only one number left, as you can see." Lana sighed and he tensed up. He'd never taken defeat well and right now he felt defeated.

He picked up the phone once more and pressed the digits. He moved his gaze to the ceiling, rocking the phone near his ear. She could hear it ring and ring. Four, six, eleven…each delay increasing his fidgeting and her tension.

"H-hello," a raspy, broken voice answered.

"Yes," Tommy began. "My name is Tommy Howell. I'm calling…"

"Hello?" Lana heard the loud, feminine voice. The person on the other end was hard of hearing.

Tommy raised his volume and spoke more slowly. "Hello… my name is Tommy Howell… "

"Tommy who?" The voice cracked. Tommy rolled his eyes, prompting Lana to grin.

"Tom…my…How…ell. I'm sorry to bother you. I'm trying to reach a man by the name of Richard Dorian, on a business matter. Is this where he lives?"

"Richard? No, Richard doesn't live here."

Tommy stood up and began pacing. "But you know Richard? Richard Dorian?"

"What? Oh yes, Richard's a cousin of mine."

Tommy looked at Lana who winked. "Did he have a charter fishing service on the Albemarle Sound?"

"Yes, that's right."

"Long-distance information gave me this number as his residence."

"Who, Richard?"

"Yes, yes," Tommy stressed. "Does your cousin Richard live there?"

"No, he doesn't," the aged voice repeated. Tommy's shoulders sagged once more, and he leaned against the table.

"Hello," the voice inquired once more. "Hello... are you there?"

"Yes... yes I'm still here," Tommy mumbled. He slumped down into his chair, resting his head on his hand. "Would you happen to know where I might reach him?" he asked in a tone of resignation.

"What?"

Tommy propped his head up with his hand and repeated the question slowly.

"Yes, yes," the voice responded, sounding a little impatient itself. "He's in the home now."

Tommy shook his head at the phone. "In what home?"

"A home for people like him."

He took a deep breath. "Can you tell me the name of the home?"

"What? Oh, yes, uh... the uh... Lifecare of Edenton."

Tommy sighed, regaining his composure. "Thank you. Thanks very much. I'm sorry to have bothered you. Have A Merry Christmas."

"Huh? What did you say?"

Tommy shook his head. "Goodbye," he said. "Thank you and Good-bye."

No sooner had he hit the Off button, than he dialed long distance info again. A moment later an operator answered.

"I need the number of a Lifecare facility in Edenton." He took another long draught of tea as he waited.

"What listing was that again," the operator requested.

Is it my imagination or can nobody hear today? "Lifecare. Lifecare of Edenton!"

"I'm sorry, sir. I don't find a listing for that. Is this a business?"

"Yes, it's a business. It's a home of some sort for elderly people. A nursing home."

"I have only one listing in that area for such a facility sir. Would you like to try that?"

He reached around to rub his neck. "I suppose I have no choice. What's the name of the place?"

"Alzheimer Care of Edenton. Hold on, I'll connect the call."

Alzheimer? *People like him. That's what the cousin said. People like him.*

Lana could see the change that the word produced in his countenance. "What's wrong?" she whispered. He held up his finger and shook his head as the phone rang.

"Hello, Alzheimer Care. How may I direct your call?"

"Patient info," Tommy stuttered. There was a pause as the call was routed to the appropriate person.

"This is Matilda Carson. Who am I speaking with? How can I help you?"

"My name is Tommy Howell. Do you have a Richard Dorian in your facility?"

"I'm sorry, sir. Are you a family member?"

Tommy hesitated. He hadn't thought about this. They weren't likely to tell him anything over the phone.

"Uh...no, not directly. Richard and my father were good friends. I just learned from uh, a cousin...oh, what was her name?"

"Cousin Martha," the staff member suggested.

"Yes, yes of course. I just learned from Martha that he's in your facility. My father died last Christmas, and we were going through some of Dad's things and Richard's name came up in some old papers, photos. We were just wondering whether he knew about my father's passing." Tommy winced, hoping this would prove satisfactory.

"Oh, I see. My apologies, sir. I hope you understand we're limited in the information we can give to non-family members."

"Oh yes, of course. I don't suppose he'd be able to remember Dad in any case. I'm puzzled about something however."

"And what is that?" The administrator inquired.

"Oh, it's probably nothing you can help me with. I was just wondering why Richard Jr. hadn't mentioned anything about his dad at our last business meeting."

"Richard Jr?" The receptionist paused. "Oh, you mean Richard A. Dorian."

"Yes, yes, Richard A. Listen I know you can't give me any info about Richard, big Richard I mean, I'm away from home, up at my Dad's house outside Destiny with all my business numbers at home in Charleston. Could you possibly give me Richard A,'s number? Would that violate company policy?"

There was a long pause, the muffle of a hand covering the mouthpiece. Then Tommy heard the clicking of computer keys in the background as the receptionist returned with a whisper.

"We aren't supposed to… since its Christmas, here's the number." She read off the digits.

"Thanks, "Tommy said. "Have a Merry Christmas!"

Tommy laid down the phone, extending his arms into the air. "Yes," He shouted.

"You found him?" Lana smiled.

"Yes, thank God! I think so and perhaps some answers to the riddle in those letters."

Chapter Thirteen

Eleven forty-five the next morning, Tommy sat drumming his fingers on the table in Sherry's Plate. He'd succeeded in contacting Richard A Dorian, who happened to be passing through Destiny on his way back from a trip. They'd agreed to meet for lunch.

A handful of the letters lay in a crumpled pile next to Tommy's glass of tea. Just a sampling, a few, very pertinent passages were included where Tommy hoped to get a little clarification for his endeavor. Richard arrived just as Sherry and Dexter joined Tommy for lunch. Tommy stood to greet him, introduced the couple seated across from him, then invited him to sit.

"Thanks so much for coming, Richard. I have a million questions."

"Glad to be of help… if I can." He glanced at his watch. "I'll have to keep a close eye on the time however."

They laughed together for a few moments amidst small talk as Richard decided what he wanted to eat. That settled, they turned their attention to the letters.

"Can you tell me what this means?" Tommy pointed to a passage about the recurring "her" in the letters. A curious expression passed over Richard's countenance. Not of surprise, more like reluctance, as though knowing the question would come, dreading the moment's arrival. Tommy's eyes narrowed when he perceived the expression. He glanced over to Sherry, whose appearance seemed to relay that she'd noted the change as well.

Richard turned up his glass, then waved towards Sherry and Dex. "I assume these are friends, close friends with whom we can talk freely."

"The closest." Tommy nodded. His guest remained silent looking down for a moment. "Richard?"

"I think I should make clear the source of the information I'm in possession of. I'm not sure

My dad would have shared any of this but when he heard your father had passed he was less guarded about confidential conversations they'd had. That and his condition. Our fathers were the best of friends, war buddies, so he knew things about your father. Much of what I know came that way. My awareness of some of the particulars is accidental."

Tommy leaned back and crossed his arms. "Okay, I understand. Tell me why you didn't mention this when you delivered the box."

"Dad's condition has been declining steadily over the past year. It isn't always easy to determine what is true and what is a product of his sickness. I didn't feel it appropriate to share. Not until or unless asked to do so. Of course I had no idea what was in the papers within the box and whether they were in any way related to the things my father had shared through the years."

"Fair enough," Tommy replied.

"Good! Now you asked about 'her.'"

"Yes. I think she's a figure in a recurring dream, but I can't make anything out beyond that."

"Mae Ling," Richard replied. "That's what our fathers, called her. Neither knew her real name, her Vietnamese name."

"Vietnamese?" Sherry leaned forward.

"Yes. Mae Ling was the name they gave a little five-year old Vietnamese child who was killed while they were in Southeast Asia together."

"What was so unusual about her?" Dex asked. Tommy looked on quietly as Richard hesitated, swallowed hard, took another drink from his glass as though washing away some bitter taste. Setting it down, he looked at the table.

"The manner in which she died."

"The way she died?" Tommy exclaimed. "How was that?"

Richard took another sip. "She was run... accidentally run over—by your father."

Sherry gasped as Tommy's lower lip quivered uncontrollably. "F-five years old?" All he could think of was little Maggie. "Run over... do you mean? What happened?"

"They were driving, Dad and Jesse, moving supplies north of Saigon. On one particular street there was a kind of celebration, or festival. The street was packed with people. Your dad was clowning around, not paying attention as they navigated the crowd. Suddenly there were screams, the vehicles following Jesse's truck started blowing their horns, shouting, waving."

Richard looked into Tommy's eyes as if assessing his strength before continuing.

"G-g-go on," Tommy urged. "What happened?"

"They climbed out of the truck, rushed back to where the crowd was gathering. There in the midst, just behind the wheels was a small girl, her body crushed, mangled. Parents were crying, some people were screaming Vietnamese obscenities at the soldiers in general, at your father in particular. According to my dad there very nearly was a riot, and real concern for your father's life."

Tommy slowly shook his head. "I never knew any of that. Never."

"Were they, er… uh… was he charged in any way?" Dexter asked.

"No." Richard looked very serious. "There was an inquiry, nothing more. Not even the civilians on the scene could give a definitive description of what'd happened. There were so many people according to my father, so much confusion and bustle; there was no way to determine what had occurred."

"Then… its likely Dad wasn't to blame," Tommy whispered.

"Entirely possible. My dad told him that a million times. For some reason, your father couldn't set the tragedy aside as a simple accident. He blamed himself. The guilt, the unnecessary self-reproach, plagued him. Dad said it affected Jesse's relationship with your mom. Maybe it did with you as well. He could never let go. After years of the recurring dream, they took to calling her Mae Ling, when they talked."

Tommy sifted through the letters locating the one which mentioned 'her and Dick.' He pointed it out to Richard. "So this Dick is your Dad?"

"That's right, Dick was his nickname," Richard affirmed. Tommy felt lightheaded, confused, afraid. He wasn't sure he could go on. His quest was proving too much for him emotionally. Finally, he sighed.

"What is it Tommy?" Sherry must have noted the despair in his eyes.

"I have a little insight into Dad's history. I understand this trauma, not how this connects to me. How did that relate to our struggles?"

They all looked at Richard. He took another sip of the tea then drew in a large breath.

"What was your favorite activity as a boy, Tommy?"

"I don't know. Comics, baseball, fishing."

"Your frequent outdoor activity?" Richard pressed.

Tommy looked up putting his hand upon his mouth. He felt sick. That gut-wrenching sensation you get when the reality of loss smacks you full bore in the face. That moment when you realize you've made a mistake and all chance of fixing it is gone forever. He could only wrestle one syllable across his lips. "War."

Richard nodded. "Yes, war. I overheard our dads conversing once, and Jesse was lamenting the fact. I didn't understand then. I thought, well, dads complaining about their kids. That was before I knew the whole story. The thing you liked doing most drove a knife in your father's heart. Every time you and your friends ran through the woods shouting '*bang, bang, bang,*' your paintball guns popping away, Jesse's insides were ripped open."

"Yes," Sherry interrupted. "I remember loaning you some money because your dad wouldn't but any paintballs for you. I thought how silly he was."

"I didn't know," Tommy protested. "I did not know! Why didn't he tell me?"

"How could he?" Dexter whispered. "How do you explain that kind of trauma to a boy?"

"When you were older, perhaps he could have," Richard suggested.

Tommy sighed, thinking back to another phrase in the letters. *How do I tell him that?* His throat grew tight: his chin fell against his chest. "By then it was too late. By the time I could've understood we were already enemies."

"Yes," Richard replied. "About the time your mother died, our dads began to drift apart. They talked less and less, leaving your dad to struggle with the secret of Mae Ling all by himself."

The air grew silent. Sherry whispered with her fiancé while Richard looked at his drink. Tommy was barely conscious of them. He was recalling some of the words his father had said in their final argument.

I was trying to teach you that things come at you out of the dark, and you have to face them. No matter how hard or frightening, you have to face them.

He'd thought his father meant the sickness that ended his life. Now he wasn't sure.

Tommy flipped through the letters, more for something to do, than in search of information. Then he recalled something Richard mentioned.

"You said our fathers drifted apart about the time my mom died?"

"Yes, that's right. Dad told me later that the fishing trip a year after her death was the last one."

Sherry studied Tommy, then reached out and touched his arm. "That was the one when he took you along, right?"

"Yes, yes it was." Tommy turned to Richard, his head propped up on his hand, and sat silently for a moment. For his part, Richard never lifted his gaze from the tea. Tommy thought he too was lost in a flood of recollections. He didn't wish to interrupt but...

"Would you know anything about why my father was unable to keep a promise he'd made to me a few days earlier?"

Richard bowed his head and began stroking his temples.

"Richard?" Tommy pressed, certain he knew something.

Richard leaned back, inhaled deeply, then laying his hand on Tommy's shoulder looked him straight in the eye...

Chapter Fourteen

Lana and Maggie sat rocking playfully in a porch swing two hours later when Lana looked up alarmed. A vehicle was speeding up the mountain road, tires squealing through every turn. A moment later she saw Tommy careen into the drive of his father's house. The gravel piled up under the tires as he slid to a stop and tumbled out of the van. *BOOM!* The door slammed behind him. Lana could tell he was seething as he stomped across the drive. Maggie leapt down, rushing to meet him.

"Look Daddy," she cried, jubilantly oblivious to the scowl on his face as she pointed to the sky. "It looks just like last year. Is it going to snow?"

The sky was lowering, a blanket of clouds growing in the whitish tint that signaled snowfall in northern climes. The air wasn't nearly cold enough however, the weather forecast silent about Christmas just two days away. Maggie knew nothing about weathermen or their predictions. She only knew what she could see and though last Christmas was her singular experience, she apparently remembered enough to know the sky had looked as it did now.

"I hope so. Promise me it's going to snow for Christmas Daddy."

Lana watched him carefully. He wasn't even looking at the child as she tugged at his pant leg.

Then he seemed to snap. "Yes, for Pete's sake yes. Yes, it's going to snow. I promise! All right? You'll get your white Christmas and be thankful. Might be the last one you'll ever see!"

Maggie drew back. The light in her eyes faded. She sulked away back to Lana. "Go play with Rachel," Lana urged.

"Tommy," she snarled after the child was gone. "What in the world? What's happened? How could you make a promise like that to your daughter?"

Stunned by his appearance Lana approached. His hair was mussed as though his fingers had run back and forth a hundred times, each journey from, or to, a different direction. His complexion flushed, eyes swollen and red. He swirled away into the house and down the hall.

Lana caught him as he reached the bedroom. She looked at him silently for a moment until he shook his head, a signal she'd learned through the years meant that he was so enraged he could not speak.

He pulled away and then fell upon the bed. She closed the door softly and watched him for a moment as he stared aimlessly at the ceiling through eyes that seemed hollow.

"Tommy?"

He pushed up on his elbows and, looked at her in a manner she hadn't seen in the past year. The old way his eyes glazed over whenever the topic of his father entered their conversations. She hadn't seen it since last year's reconciliation. What could have given it rebirth?

"Lana," he finally said. "I love you. I cannot talk now. Please leave me alone, and I will be all you want me to be for the children in a while." His words were cold, stern. He fell back upon the bed without another sound, and she withdrew.

He was as good as his pledge however, emerging from the bedroom two hours later just as they were about to call him to supper. His face newly shaved, his raven locks restrained once more. He leaned over to kiss Lana's cheek lightly before taking his seat next to her. Maggie on his other side, took his hand gently as they paused to return thanks for the meal.

John as the oldest of Tommy's siblings,

and since the death of Jesse, head of this clan, offered the prayer and with "Amen," the table was filled with the clatter of plates and conversation. There was no mention of Tommy's interview with Richard Dorian. The dinner went smoothly, with laughter-filled memories. The only things distracting Lana was Maggie's persistent sharing of the promised snow with cousin Rachel, and Tommy's subdued manner. Afterwards, there was punch, cookies, eggnog, and a Christmas favorite in the DVD player. About ten, the children scattered to their bedrooms, and the adults separated into couples, engaging in soft conversations. Lana questioned Tommy on his interview with Mr. Dorian.

"Well?" She pressed.

"Well what?"

"Oh Tommy, please. What did you learn from Mr. Dorian? What got you so upset? Or didn't he show up?"

"Oh no!" Tommy jerked his head back and forth. "No, he was there all right and full of information too. He shed light on a number of questions. Very helpful, quite instructive indeed."

Lana's eyebrows knit together. She drew back from him, laying her hand on her chin. "So, if he was helpful why this tone? Didn't he give you enough time to make your inquiries?"

"No, no," Tommy replied curtly. "He was more than willing for all the time I needed. So promising was his help that I invited him to join

Sherry and Dexter with us tomorrow evening to discuss things further. Of course, that was before…" He stopped short, catching himself—but it was too late. His rising voice had disrupted the conversation of the others.

"That was before what Tommy?"

He jumped up, walked into the kitchen, then returned and leaned against the back of the couch, as though in pain. "That was before I asked him about why Dad broke his promise, the promise about the fishing trip."

Lana nodded while the others all looked at each other quizzically. He'd mentioned a promise the other day but hadn't explained. Tommy seemed unable or unwilling to tell his siblings about the encounter at the overlook, so Lana gave them a quick overview.

"So," Dina urged. "What did he say about that?"

"I'm almost embarrassed to tell you what he insinuated," Tommy fumed. "It's… so unbelievable. I couldn't restrain myself. The very idea!"

Lana reached over and laid her hand upon his. "What idea?

Tommy took a deep breath, struggling to control his emotions. "He said… that the reason Dad broke his promise to me was… was because… Dear God! I'm … still too angry to … discuss…"

"Take a breath," Dina suggested. "Breathe and tell us what happened."

"He told me... the reason... Dad failed to keep his promise was because... of news he learned that day... that day, when he told me the weather was too rough to go fishing!"

His voice was rising and broken as the others looked on.

"Go on Tommy," Dina urged as Wayne agreed.

"Yes Tommy, get it out. Let us help you with this."

"He told me..." Tommy paused, pulling a handkerchief from his pocket and wiping his eyes. "He told me th—that...that Dad learned Mom had been unfaithful to him."

"Unfaithful?" Dina leaned forward from the chair. "Mom?"

"Yes!" Tommy roared. "Can you believe that?' He waved a fist in the air, pounded the couch. "I was two seconds from striking him right then and there, if not for Sherry restraining me. The nerve—making such an accusation against my mother. Blaming Mom for Dad's failure to keep a promise."

"Tommy... why... why would he say such a thing," Lana asked, "Unless..."

"Un...! Unless what?" he shouted. "What are you trying to say?" Lana shook her head. She glanced around the room and everyone looked shocked, surprised— except for John. She saw his odd expression, and figured Tommy would as well, but rage seemed to be blinding him.

Wayne interrupted the angry eruption. "But Tommy, why wouldn't you believe what he said?"

"His father has dementia, that's why! Richard himself said the only reason he learned these things is his dad told him in periods when his memory wasn't clear. This had to be one of those moments."

"Then why invite him over?" Wayne pressed.

"I extended the in-invitation before that…accusation."

Sally who'd been silent sounded doubtful. "You aren't going to follow through are you?"

John cleared his throat. Lana saw him look at Sally then shake his head slightly. A look passed between them. The kind of unspoken interaction that occurs between husband and wife. Lana wondered why John should be so mysterious.

"I don't know," Tommy snapped, running his fingers through his hair, mussing the raven mane once more. "There are more questions I could ask, want to—*need* to ask." He stopped, took a long breath. "I just don't think I can face him again. Not after that."

"You have no choice Tommy."

Everyone looked about to see John, who'd risen and stepped over to the window. He did not turn to face them as he spoke.

"What do you mean I have no choice?" Tommy challenged.

"If you want to learn anything more about those letters, you have no other option. You'll have to query Richard Dorian."

Tommy was livid once more by this time, very much the same as Lana had seen him when he entered the house hours earlier. He took a step in John's direction clenching and unclenching his fists. Lana feared the years of antagonism between them might get out of control.

"What do you mean I have no options? I sure do. I don't have to listen to those kinds of accusations! Why should I listen to that kind of charge?"

John turned slowly from the window. "Because it's true."

Chapter Fifteen

Lana gasped as she turned to Tommy. She could feel his pain. His lips moved without sound as the color drained from his face. He stood frozen a moment more. No one in the room uttered a word. He swallowed hard.

"H—how, how could you say such a thing? It's not so! Say it isn't true."

"I can't." John looked down and shoved his hands in his pockets, scraping his feet on the floor.

Tommy turned toward Dina, then to Lana shaking his head, mouthing the word "no." Lana was shaken by the look in his eyes. They seemed soulless, as if his inner being had been ripped out leaving only two dark cavities where his pupils once lay. She couldn't find sufficient words for such despair.

Tommy scuffed around and collapsed onto the couch next to Lana, who wrapped one hand around his back weaving the other through his arm. His hands were clenched and white from his straining grip. He trembled slightly, and shook his head repeatedly as Lana looked on.

Finally, he pushed off the couch and started across the room toward his brother.

"I can't believe what I'm hearing," he exclaimed. "Why would you say such a thing? How would you even know something like that? How could you?"

John, his head still hung low, shuffled across the room and took his seat again by Sally. Tommy stepped toward his brother with a menacing look. Lana wanted to console her husband, but he left her no opportunity.

"John!" He blasted. "I asked you a question. How could you know such a thing?"

John looked up slowly, his own eyes full of tears. "Because Mom told me."

Tommy's mouth eased open again, and his shoulders slumped. "What did you say?"

John looked over at Dina, who, though

quiet, had the same look of disbelief on her face. He nodded lightly. "She *told* me."

Tommy stood silent, a wild, confused gleam in his eye. Lana rose, walked to his side, then led him to the couch once more.

"When?" Dina took up the interrogation. "When did she tell you that?"

John wiped away his tears. "About a year before she died. We were down in Destiny for some reason, and she'd been depressed, more than usual. All of a sudden as we were driving along, she began to tell me about how she'd failed Dad. I didn't understand her at first. I thought she meant... you know because of the way Dad always rode her. I thought she just didn't feel like a good enough wife."

He stopped for a moment, his voice breaking. Sally hugged him, encouraging him. "Go on."

"I remember she talked about how Dad was always accusing her of unfaithfulness. You remember the endless arguments they had. Then out of the blue, she told me. Those were *her* words, 'I've only been unfaithful once.' I know its hard Tommy." John sniffled. "I've argued with myself—hoped—through the years that she meant something else. It isn't anything I'd forget," he declared defiantly, then softened his tone. "I remember feeling very uneasy. I don't think I even believed it myself until now."

"What ... did you s-say to her?" Tommy

whispered.

"I'm ashamed to tell you." John shook his head and rose, pacing across the floor between the stove and the window. "I told her I—I didn't want to hear it. I didn't feel comfortable. What? Was I supposed to be her priest? No child can serve in that role. I felt bad, for her, for myself. I didn't know what to say. So I asked her not to tell me anything more."

The group grew quiet except for the thud of John's steps. Finally he halted and whirled to face his brother.

"You see, Tommy. You aren't the only person with painful memories."

Tommy breathed in sharply at the rebuke as though a knife had penetrated his heart. Lana could sense how hurt he was.

"Why didn't you ever tell us?" Dina interrupted.

"Tell you! What the devil did you want me to say? 'Hey guys Mom cheated on Dad.' I didn't even want to hear it myself. How could I tell you?"

"You're telling us now," Wayne offered.

"Yes! Yes, I am and quite against my will. I never would have said it. I would've gladly lied to myself for the rest of my life. That I had misunderstood, that it couldn't be true, not about her... not my mom." He extended his arm toward the box. "How was I to know someday a mysterious ... container ... full of letters would bring the revelation to light? How?"

"Who was it?" Tommy muttered almost unintelligibly. "What was the man's name?"

John put his hand to his head. "I don't know, Tommy. The conversation went no further. I …" He stumbled a moment, his voice wavering and broken. "I guess she wanted to get it off her chest and had no one else to tell. In spite of my disbelief, I've always regretted that I failed her in that."

"No," Tommy said, regaining his composure. He rose violently from the couch. "No! I won't believe this. Not Mom. Not my mother! Dad was the villain in this family, not Mom. Not Mom!"

"Tommy," Wayne began. "You can't deny the truth as offered by Mr. Dorian and your own brother."

"Oh yes, I can," Tommy replied defiantly. "The Dorians did not know my mother."

"And John?" Sally protested. "What about him?"

"He's wrong too! Don't ask me how," he said waving his hand in anticipation of the objection. "I don't know how, he just is."

John pulled the handkerchief away from his face and stood. "That's so like you, Tommy. The world's so black and white to you. Dad was the villain, Mom the saint."

"I don't think she was a saint. But I won't let you insult her like this."

"What? Won't what? Won't let me insult her? Do you think you're the only person who cared about her?" John challenged. "I repeat… you thought she was a saint. Your anger toward Dad was so sharp you couldn't see her humanity."

"I never thought she was a saint."

"Oh yes you did! You still do. Why else would you refuse to accept the fact that she was human? That Dad's coldness and verbal abuse might have driven her to the unthinkable; to seek some solace in the arms of another. Only someone who thought her a saint could exclude the possibility that she was human. Empty and alone most of the time, she reached out to fill the void. I'm not justifying it—I'm explaining it to you. Don't stand there and tell me I'm wrong. She told me, *me!*"

"Why?" Tommy yelled. Lana trembled as she noted the contempt that Tommy had always struggled with concerning John. His eyes filled with rage. "Why would she tell you that?"

"I don't know!" John shouted back. Sally tugged on his sleeve and he softened his tone, sliding back into his chair. "I don't know, Tommy. But she did. It happened whether you like it or not. I don't know what you said to Mr. Dorian, or whether you'll still have him come with your friends tomorrow evening. If you do— apologize. He told you the truth."

John took Sally by the arm, and they

walked silently from the room. Tommy slumped back onto the couch once more and cast a questioning stare in Dina's direction. She shook her head sadly.

"John wouldn't lie to us Tommy. There's no reason he should. Not about this."

Tommy's face fell into his hands. He didn't sob but the staggered, guttural sounds revealed what great effort he expended not to.

Lana nudged him a few moments later. She was wondering whether Tommy's encounter had ever gotten back to his dilemma about the overlook commitment. "What did Mr. Dorian say, honey? About your dad's promise?"

He took a breath, clearly fighting to speak. "A-par... apparently Dad over...heard the man talking to uh...a friend. Someone from the other party we were supposed to go out on the Sound with."

"Did Richard know what they said?" Dina whispered.

"No. Not word for word, only what his father shared with him, what he told him of the details of the event."

"And what did he say?" Lana pressed. Tommy inhaled deeply, running his hands through his hair repeatedly.

"He s-said Dad... over...overheard the men talking. The guy called...uh, mom's name, mentioned where she lived. Couldn't have been anyone else. Dad was so infuriated that he refused to go out fishing with them and made Dick Dorian call off the trip on the pretext of the conditions. Though he gave in to dad's demands out of respect for their friendship, it ended the relationship."

He cried now, tears freely flowing interrupted by broken words and phrases that were difficult for the others to interpret or decipher, except for one:

"I wish to God I had never been given that box!"

Lana whispered. "You don't mean that Tommy."

"Yes." He nodded vigorously. "I do mean it! I wanted to understand Dad not have my heart ripped out. Not have Mom's memory stained—slandered. What good is this? In heaven's name, how can this possibly help?"

Lana brushed back his hair. "I know it's hard to accept now, with the wound fresh in your heart. So I remind you, it helps because now you know it wasn't just a failure on your father's part to ignore his vow. You've seen he was sincere in his desire to make things right. Remember what he said about things coming out of the dark? Maybe he was thinking about this. Maybe he was trying to apologize for never explaining why he broke… no…" Lana glanced around at Dina searching for the right words. "No, why he *couldn't* keep that promise."

"Mom had been dead a year when dad made that promise, Lana," Tommy protested. "Why take it out on me? It wasn't my fault?"

Dina leaned in. "You're not being fair, Tommy. What'd you expect him to say? 'I'm sorry son, I found out your mother betrayed me.' John's right. It's not always that simple."

Lana stood, still holding Tommy's hand. "Let's go to bed and get some rest. You need it."

"No. No, I'll stay up a bit. I couldn't sleep just now. I need to think some of this over."

Lana knew where he was going. "Well, while you're thinking, remember what you said on Thanksgiving Day and just now? You wanted to understand your dad. What made him so cold, difficult? You've found something that caused him great pain. Try to understand that part of the man. Okay?"

Tommy nodded, smiling, then kissed her hand as she pulled away. Wayne and Dina also withdrew after Dina offered a sisterly pat on his head.

**

Tommy went into the kitchen for a drink. After throwing in a pine log he moved his chair close to the stove. He sat, lost in the throes of his mental wrestling. The arteries of his spiritual heart, flushed clear a year ago by forgiveness, were constricting. Though he despised the suggestion, John was right. Tommy had viewed his mother as a saint, and rightly so. His father was the demon in that relationship. Whatever hurt she'd caused his father was deserved. Tommy tapped his feet and ground his teeth as the bitterness grew.

Then he caught himself. It's Christmas. And hadn't he promised to be what his family needed? He had to find a way to turn his attention to sweeter things if he had any hope of rest. He reached over, grabbed the television remote, and clicked play on the DVD. As the screen came to life he was greeted by faces he barely recognized.

What? This isn't the Christmas movie they were watching earlier...this is... why that's the home movie Lana had discovered among the letters. Who is...that?

Tommy watched as a figure, a strangely familiar, slender man jumped down off an embankment into the camera's view. A lump formed in his throat— it was Jesse, his father, like Tommy had never seen him before. Young, active, happy. He was teasing someone behind the camera, not the individual recording the scene, another person. His mom perhaps. But that was definitely his father, a version of his dad he couldn't remember—or had chosen not to. His dad's face was brilliant with delight.

Tommy choked back emotion, struggled to withhold his tears. He longed to know that Jesse, to talk to him once more. To feel the stubble of his beard, the cackle of his laugh. He wiped away the tears that were blurring the unrecognized scenery.

A child wandered into the frame and the man lifted and threw the young boy into the air. He fell back into the father's arms. Tommy broke into a huddle of sobs. The boy was himself. Animated by laughter, happier than he'd ever remembered being, and with a father equally blissful over his son. Tommy wiped his eyes and tried to regain his composure lest he disturb the others as the scene played on. Though there was no sound, the filmmaker followed the man and his son a moment until the camera turned in a different direction and he saw...

Mom... smiling, happy. *What happened to that family?*

He rehashed all that he'd heard lately, pondering the pledge his father made then broke, and why. In the jumble of his thought, he recalled something Richard had said about Tommy's preoccupation with playing war, how Dad felt about that. Tommy shifted.

How that must have hurt. *Funny...I'd never thought of Dad as a weak hurting person. He was hard, mean, that's the Jesse I knew and could go on believing in...if not for this film. He was human after all, broken like all of us...like me.* Wounded by out of control events, unseen things coming out of the dark.

Tommy was swept away by Jesse's anguish. Crushed by the full impact of the role he'd played. How often in those verbal sparring matches had he uttered something about his mom? Wishing she'd lived, that his father had died. How much better life would've been without him? Tommy heard his angry voice hurling those hateful barbs, each one dredging up a pain Jesse could not share nor hide from. How he wished he could take them all back.

"I'm sorry, Dad. I'm so sorry. I know you can't hear me, but I wish I could've understood events behind the breaking of your promise. Maybe things would have been different."

The emotional torrent subsided and he realized how exhausted he was from this day's emotional roller coaster. He made his way to the bedroom, sure that he would rest. But he was plagued by the power of promises, and the need to honor them. He remembered his own word to Maggie. How could he keep his commitment and give her a white Christmas?

Chapter Sixteen

Lana was in the kitchen early the next morning working to bake fresh strawberry muffins without waking everyone in the house, especially Tommy. She'd wakened when he climbed in next to her and glancing at the clock saw it was extremely late. She tried extra hard not to disturb him when she rose. She was sipping on a cup of cocoa when Maggie shuffled into the room.

"What's wrong, Magpie?" Maggie pointed to the window. Lana looked out, noticing nothing peculiar. She leaned over and inquired again. "I don't know what you're pointing at Maggie."

"I'm pointing at the sun," she whimpered. "It isn't snowing like Daddy promised it would."

Lana straightened up with a sigh. "Yes, well Daddy should not have done that. He was distressed about grown-up things and wasn't thinking when he made that very unwise statement. He'll apologize today."

Her words of rebuke did nothing to lessen Maggie's dismay as she climbed into a chair, her lips drawn into a pout, her head resting on one hand.

"Would you like something to eat?"

"I guess," Maggie replied sullenly.

"Cereal or muffin?" Lana held out each. Maggie nodded toward the cereal and Lana poured a bowl and set it before her just as John and Sally walked into the kitchen. They exchanged morning greetings for a few moments and discussed plans for the day until Maggie finished her breakfast and wandered off again.

"Tommy still in bed?" John sipped on his coffee and eyed Lana.

"Yes." Lana nodded then sat down. "I don't know whether he's sleeping but he's in bed. He came in rather late. Probably up thinking again about the news."

John looked across at Lana, his face drawn tight with seriousness. "I was surprised he took it so hard."

Lana's head twitched, and her ire rose as she returned the gaze of her brother-in-law. "Surprised?" she exclaimed. "Why in the world would you be? I know you guys were never close, but surely you can understand how that made him feel."

"I don't think John has ever understood Tommy, Lana."

"I'm sure you're right, Sally. I don't always understand Tommy. Still, even if you knew it were possible, that isn't the kind of news anyone would welcome. You had a much better relationship with Jesse and yet you yourself said you found it hard to believe. Think about how hard it was for Tommy."

John looked down. "I'm sorry. I didn't intend to sound so uncaring. I simply meant that it was so long ago. Mom's been gone almost twenty years. I couldn't imagine it would be that big a deal to him now, that's all I was trying to say."

Lana sat back in her chair. "I see your point. You have to remember that for most of his adult life at least, Tommy looked at your father as the bad guy, the one who always failed. Your mom, fairly or not, became his heroine. And after she was gone? Well… memories, especially the ones connected to lost family members, have a tendency to morph. Quite unintentionally, to use your language, your mom became a saint. Last night your confirmation of Richard Dorian's revelation struck down the only thing Tommy's held dear from his childhood."

John looked up and gazed softly at Lana for a moment as Sally looked on. "I … uh, never considered that. What else could I do? Have Tommy continue his rant against Richard Dorian without cause?"

Sally refilled his coffee. "No one's suggesting that, dear."

"Of course not," Lana replied. "Perhaps waiting till he got all of his anger out might have been better."

"I guess so. But it's done now."

"What's done?" a bleary-eyed Tommy asked as he stepped into the kitchen. John was clearing his throat when Lana interrupted him. "The coffee," she said pouring Tommy a cup. "This is as fresh as can be."

He mussed his hair and shook his head. "I'll need a lot. I've a thousand cobwebs upstairs today." His eyes were bloodshot and puffy. He took the cup Lana offered and swallowed two large gulps even though steam was swirling up from the mug.

John cleared his throat. "Tommy, I… I'm sorry about last night. We were just talking and I… could have told you that news differently. Perhaps not at all."

"Not at all?" Tommy chuckled, though without much humor. "No… no you were right. I needed to know. I wanted to learn what made Dad and my relationship so difficult. Maybe the two things I discovered yesterday were too much."

"Two things?" Lana brushed back his hair.

"What was the other?"

They listened as he told them the story of Mae Ling and how Tommy's childhood preoccupation with war had probably been a source of heartache for Jesse.

"I thought all night about it," Tommy continued. "I can see now that my devotion to Mom served the same purpose. I never realized how much pain I caused him. I didn't mean to."

"No one's blaming you— except you Tommy."

"I know, baby. I just wonder if things could have been different, if I had known. If I only could've known."

"All of us have painful secrets Tommy." Wayne had joined them about midway through his brother-in-law's Mae Ling explanation. "I remember something about an uncle of mine. He was my favorite relative, jovial, funny, and inventive. He gave me a Coast Guard flag, and baseball bats that he said he got in New York, and a very large parachute. I remember when I first heard about the parachute, I thought he was bringing me the real thing. I went up the steps of our house and wondered if it was high enough to jump from there. It turned out to be only a toy." They all burst out with laughter.

"He always made me cackle," Wayne continued. "He was adventurous, always living somewhere exotic, at least in my mind. California, Florida, France. He gave off an air of confidence, was successful, you'd have never thought he'd endured any kind of pain. Then a great aunt told me about when his mother died. He was only five, she heard him cry out in the darkness, 'my mommy died tonight.'"

They were silent as Wayne sighed and sipped coffee. "I always looked at him differently after that. I felt… well as if I had somehow failed him by not being aware of that pain." Wayne reached up and wiped his nose and Lana smiled while Dina, who had joined them now, rubbed his shoulders.

"Anyway my point is, everybody has secret pain. Some of which we'll never know. We could've only done something if we'd known."

They all nodded and mumbled their agreement. They sat for a while longer sipping coffee and talking about the coming celebration.

"Christmas morning?" Tommy jumped up from his seat. "Tomorrow *is* Christmas Eve. And I've got a ton of things to do before Dexter and Sherry arrive tonight." He looked at John. "Are you and Sally still taking the kids to that church festival as planned?"

"Yes we are," Sally beamed. "We're very excited."

"Good," Tommy replied, pausing to take a long draught of the coffee. "That will allow us some quality time for our friends."

"Yes." Lana pushed away from the table and stood, clearing her throat. "Speaking of 'quality time...'" she said sternly. "You should think of spending some with Maggie. This glorious December sunshine has her in quite a mood due to the ill-conceived promise of a certain father figure. How in the world are you going to explain this?" She put one hand on her hip and glared at Tommy. He grimaced and nodded, then turned to his coffee.

"Tommy Howell. What are you going to do?"

"I don't know, but I have two days to think of something. Avoid the topic if you can with her—and me—until I figure this out. Okay?"

Lana nodded because there was little else she could do. She didn't want any more diminishing of the Christmas spirit than Tommy's search had already caused. All she could do was pray silently.

Dear God please give us a miracle of Christmas snow—for Maggie's sake.

Chapter Seventeen

Tommy stepped back and surveyed the preparations Lana had just finished around the room when the headlamps of their guest's cars shone through the picture window. Candles were lit on the table, the air smelled of cedar and cinnamon, the tree lights twinkled magically in the soft illumination, while Christmas carols sung by Bing Crosby wafted through the air.

Sherry and Dexter entered first, then Richard made his way up the walk and onto the porch. Tommy swallowed hard as he approached. He greeted Richard with as much civility as he could muster given his previous tirade. Tommy quickly gathered up the coats and carried them to the bedroom.

"Let me offer my congratulations on your engagement, Sherry," Lana offered as they hugged. "That's such great news. I wish you both great happiness." Lana turned and shook hands with Dexter before turning her attention to Richard.

"Hello, I'm Richard Dorian. My friends call me Rick."

Lana extended her hand. "It's good to meet you as well. Please come in and make yourself at home."

"I wasn't sure I'd still be welcome after the difficult news I've had to share with Tommy."

"Punch anyone?" Tommy interrupted.

"Think nothing of it. He feels bad enough for both of you," Lana continued as Richard followed her into the dining area.

Dexter preferred wine and helped himself as Tommy was dipping punch for those who'd raised their hands at his inquiry. Lana sidled up next to him.

"Don't you have something to say, Tommy?"

"About?"

"Your regrets over yesterday." Lana raised her brow.

"Ah." Tommy nodded. "Yes about that, Richard. I…uh, I—I owe you an apology, for my behavior. The revelation was more of a shock than I was prepared for. I wanted info about Dad.

I never dreamed my image of Mom would be challenged in the process."

"I understand. I hope we can continue to be friends in spite of those tidings."

"Of course," Tommy said, patting his shoulder. "Now, we have various finger foods and desserts here so help yourself. I'll have some of these miniature stuffing balls and gravy dip myself."

Everyone laughed as he loaded about ten onto his plate, then made small talk over the selection of foods and sugary treats. Tommy kept a sharp eye on the punch bowl as this was his favorite holiday drink. In addition there was eggnog, and hot chocolate, so he felt confident they'd have all they desired.

After a while, the food and desserts trays sat idle, and the light atmosphere grew more subdued as they settled on the couch and chairs around the fire. In casual conversation the topic wound around at last to the box and Tommy's search.

"Have you given any more thought to that last revelation?" Dexter poured himself another serving of wine.

Tommy set down his glass and tossed another log into the stove. "Quite a bit. My brother John confirmed what you'd said Rick." He looked over and winked. "If you think I was rough on you, you should have seen me then."

Lana mouthed the words "not pretty," to

which they all giggled, including Tommy.

"So what now, Tommy?" Dexter leaned forward. "What do you do with the letters and the chest they came in?"

"I'm not sure, Dex." Tommy's effort at restraining his emotions was becoming difficult, his volume falling again. He gestured toward Rick. "Richard was certain the box was meant for me. He unknowingly delivered it at a time when I wanted to understand Dad's character, his abrupt manners. Still, I don't know how to move forward. Maybe I need some time to digest what's there, study more of the letters. That will have to wait of course. The quest has already stolen a lot of our Christmas joy."

"Well," Lana spoke up in that manner that he knew was intended to cheer him up. "So far, we know that your dad suffered an enormous tragedy, unlike anything most of us will endure. And he experienced a great betrayal that might have been related, actually."

Sherry, who had been gazing into the fire, turned now to Lana. "What do you mean exactly?"

"Let's see. I think that the distance— Jesse's inability to deeply love his family, aided in part by the Mae Ling tragedy— played into the emptiness that Tommy's mom felt. The unrequited love that drove her, perhaps regrettably, if we take John's words to heart, to try to fill that void in another man's arms, was a product of Jesse's anguish." Lana glanced over at Richard. "I wonder whether she knew, about Mae Ling I mean."

Rick took a sip of punch then shook his head. "I don't know about that. My guess would be no. The way my dad spoke suggested it was his and Jesse's secret and no one else's, other than their fellow soldiers at the time. However, I can see your point, Lana. Who knows what that kind of secret would do to someone's heart?"

"You'd think he'd have gotten some kind of counseling from the military," Dexter observed.

"Dad?" Tommy chuckled. "No... not my dad. Apparently, he never even shared it with the woman he chose to marry. I doubt if he'd have submitted to counseling, to sharing those things with a complete stranger."

"Makes you wonder," Sherry mused.

Tommy turned to this lifelong friend, feeling a warmth inside. Somehow it was right that she should be here, helping as she'd done so many times through their childhood years. "Wonder about what?"

"Oh... all the little things that shape us. How we came to be the persons we are today. How many people out there have hidden trauma, a secret pain holding them back? Skewing what other people think of them. What they think about themselves."

They nodded as the mood grew somber.

Tommy sighed. "Hiders."

"Hiders?" Dexter looked at the others. "What in the world does that mean?"

Tommy sipped on his punch before answering. "It's a phrase a pastor friend of mine uses, about people. He calls them hiders because they keep things— hidden. They're frightened, so very afraid to let people in behind the veil. Their fear has taught them how to protect themselves behind a wall of secrecy. They know who to say what to, the right answers, to keep people at bay, or to fit in without being exposed. Intimidated into never being completely honest about anything—anyone. I never thought of Dad that way. He was always outgoing, gregarious, much like the description my brother-in-law Wayne gave us of his uncle. I suppose it should teach us never to make judgments based on how strong someone seems."

"We help people from the inside out," Sherry offered. "Or… at least that's how we should help them."

Dexter bowed. "Yes, but how do you get inside of a hider, as Tommy calls them?"

"I wonder what other secrets he was hiding," Lana mused.

Tommy's heart quivered. There was a sudden sick, sucking feeling in the middle of his belly as though his insides were being drawn out and laid on the floor to be trampled on. He pondered how close he'd come to letting the old anger resurface last night. What he felt now was pity.

His father had never been a tyrant by choice. He, like everyone else, was broken, wounded. Nowhere to turn, none to understand. In an age when men were expected to be strong, invincible, Jesse had no one to cry with, or comprehend his hurts and disappointments.

Tommy fought back tears in the rush of emotions. He left the room on a pretense for a moment, then returned a few minutes later when the conversation had turned to other things.

"Well," Dexter remarked as he looked at his watch. "Nine thirty. I think we should be going."

"Must you? So soon?" Tommy protested.

"I'm afraid so." Sherry rose from the couch. "We're catering our first Christmas Eve dinner tomorrow, and I've a ton of work to do in preparation. Thanks for having us. This was a great time of fellowship. Thanks for letting us be part of your family. Sorry we have to leave."

"I'll get your coats," Lana offered.

"I guess I'll be going also." Richard stood and stretched. "I'll be driving over to Edenton first thing in the morning. How about you guys? Taking things easy tomorrow, I suppose?"

"For the most part." Lana returned with the jackets. "Most of our preparation is done— other than the exception of one major obstacle."

Tommy felt her glare as she spoke.

"That sounds rather ominous, Tommy," Richard replied. "What's up? Anything I can do to help?"

"Not unless you can control the weather."

"What?" Dexter helped Sherry with her coat. "What does the weather have to do with it?"

Tommy looked over at Lana and shrugged before she explained.

"When Tommy came back yesterday, Rick, from your first… encounter shall we say… bearing the news you'd given him about his mother, he was so angry he made a rather rash oath to a certain child about a white Christmas. And now he has to tell the child how stupid that promise was."

They murmured as Tommy nodded his agreement and led them to the door. All but Richard, that is. Tommy felt that sense that Rick was being mysterious again, like when they'd first met. Tommy assumed Rick's mind was drifting to the difficult day he'd have with his father tomorrow and on Christmas Day. When they got to the door and shook hands, Richard hesitated. There was one of those "I've something I need to say" looks on his face. But the sensation passed as they hugged and wished *Merry Christmas* before their guests made their way to the cars, Tommy and Lana waving from the door.

Chapter Eighteen

Though Tommy had thought long and hard through the night, mingling his musings with ample pleas for divine intervention, morning brought no easy answer to his predicament. He had neither a plan for keeping his word nor the courage to look into the delicate orbs of his daughter and break her heart. He hoped Lana would have an overabundance of Christmas spirit and take the poison for him.

"Oh no you don't, Tommy Howell." She huffed at his first suggestion. "My Christmas is not about to be ruined by your stupidity and cowardice. You made the pledge, you have to be the one who tells her why the promise can't be kept."

"Lana, how can I possibly do that? That'll break her heart."

"Great conclusion, Captain Obvious. And waking up tomorrow without snow won't? You should have thought of that before."

He turned away, poured another cup of coffee, and sipped a minute before going on. "Yes, you're right I should have... but you know now that my... my uh... mind wasn't focused on doing the right thing at the moment."

Lana followed as he sat down by the fire. She drew near, running her fingers through his raven locks.

"I understand, and I sympathize with how much that had to hurt. I wish it would've happen--ed at a different time. I don't know what you can do except to tell Maggie how snow happens and apologize for your lack of control—over the weather and your tongue. I'm going to get dressed."

As she sauntered off, Tommy rose and placed another log in the stove then stood by the window. Another source of sadness rose in his heart as he gazed through the glass.

So it's arrived. The final Christmas at home. The last time this family will sing carols and open presents and celebrate the birth of Christ on this mountainside. The last time... the very last time.

Tommy had had moments when memories rushed by like a mountain stream, roaring and foaming with the spring melt of winter. Echoes too fast and abundant to detail or express, overflowing with emotion. Some cheerful, others poignant, all valuable and life shaping. So he remained in the warm, silent, sunshine, lost in these thoughts until he heard a shuffle behind him. Turning, he was yanked into the present moment of distress—there stood Maggie. He swallowed hard.

"Magpie," he exclaimed as gathered her up. "My, don't you look beautiful this morning. Today is Christmas Eve. This time tomorrow you'll be opening presents and sharing the ones you brought for your cousins and for Aunt Dina. Won't that be great?"

Maggie seemed unimpressed with his jubilance. "I guess so," she muttered.

He gulped. "Would you like something to eat?"

She shook her head, her eyes downcast, lips pouting.

You can't leave her like this Tommy. They were his thoughts, but he was sure they were in Lana's stern tone of voice. *I'll get this over with now and give her the rest of the day to recover.*

"Uh listen, Magpie…"

"Yes, Daddy," she murmured, her voice tinged with a sadness that sent shudders through his soul.

"Well… Magpie… sometimes grown-ups do stupid things. They uh… they say things they shouldn't say."

She nodded. "And make promises they can't keep."

Ouch!

"Yes, Magpie that's right. And when they do, the grown-up thing to do is apologize. Now… for example… I made a vow to you and… well that was a stupid thing to do… because…"

Just then his ringtone sounded. *Saved—for a moment at least.*

"I wonder who that can be this time of morning. Excuse me a moment Magpie, okay?"

She slid out of his lap as he made his way to the phone, while holding his finger in the air and avoiding eye contact with Lana who'd reappeared a moment earlier,

"One minute and then… hello."

"Tommy, its Rick. I hope I didn't wake you."

"Hey Rick. No you didn't. We've been up a while. What's up?"

"I had an idea last night before I left and I was hesitant to bring it up."

"Really? You know I discussed that with Lana last night after you'd gone. So what was the important thing you forgot to mention? Yes. Why… why that's a great idea!" Tommy chuckled and gave Lana a thumbs up. "Your sister you say? Yes, let me get a pen."

Tommy wrote down the number as Lana scowled. "Richard, thank you. Wow! That is an answer to prayer. I can't thank you enough. Yes, yes you too. Have a Merry Christmas. Okay, good-bye."

Suddenly free of his guilt and predicament, Tommy turned to Lana and Magpie.

He walked over to where they sat, and looked Maggie in the eye. "Magpie. Daddy is going to keep his commitment. You, my precious little one, you will have a white Christmas. I promise. It has to be our secret okay?"

Maggie smiled then skipped cheerfully away. Lana's mouth caverned.

"The faith of a child is almost as magical as Christmas itself," Tommy observed.

"Tommy. What in the world are you…?"

Tommy put his finger on her lips. "Trust me on this. Remember what I said last night about Richard having that look? Seems I was right. He didn't want to say anything until he'd called his sister and checked out his idea. He gave me the way to fulfill that pledge."

"And what did he tell you exactly?" Lana put her hands on her hips, curiosity gleaming from her eyes.

"He told me this…"

Chapter Nineteen

Tommy stole into Maggie's bedroom about eleven-thirty that night, after sneaking out to start the van. He slipped his arms under her body, lifted her gently from the bed, and carried her into the living room. She murmured slightly as he pulled her sweater and coat over her pajamas, and her socks and boots onto her feet. Then he picked her up and lugged her through the door to the warm van, which was purring softly. After snugging her in the car seat he went back into the house, pulled a large gift from under the tree and returned laying it on the front seat. Maggie was pouting when he climbed into his own seat.

"What's wrong Magpie?"

"There's no snow, Daddy. You promised me a white Christmas."

"Do you trust me?" She nodded. "Then sit back and hang on. It's okay to go back to sleep but remember when I tell you to, you've agreed to close your eyes and keep them shut until I say so. Right?"

Maggie snuggled down into her coat. Tommy knew she'd be out long before their destination. He pulled out of the drive before putting on the lights, then made his way down the hill where his childhood years were spent. About a half hour trek lay before them until they arrived at the location where Tommy had arranged to keep his promise. Maggie's deep breathing assured him she was sound asleep again and the surprise would not be ruined. Then his mind drifted.

Easily done, for the route was as plain in his mind's eye as anything he could think of. So plain he was puzzled he hadn't thought of Richard's solution himself. How simple it was. But then it hadn't been an issue until two days ago, with his ill-advised promise.

He'd traveled this road…what? A thousand times. Probably not that many, still it seemed so as he thought back over the years.

There was the overlook where the promise that had haunted him so long was made. A year ago the spot was a sore point, a festering wound on his heart from which only despair could be seen. Now through clarity—the painful clarity of understanding—he could see again. The lights of Destiny sparkled clear and pristine in the valley below.

He could feel the cold beyond the van's interior against the window's glass, air crisp with late December's bite. How strange that as he passed Sherry's childhood home his thoughts were filled with sweaty summer nights when they played and laughed in her yard. A hundred images jumbled together in a moment's recollection. Days at the pool, waiting on the porch till a thunderstorm passed.

Then past the ballpark. Silent in the winter darkness, dead. Spring would green the grass. Cheering parents and jeering opponents would fill the stands. His first real summer job of marking the lines and dragging the infield for the softball games. The source of so much of his mother's loneliness, the site of his painful Naismith story. There could only be one word capable of describing the emotions evoked—bittersweet.

Summer drives home from the ballpark in the back of his dad's pickup, snuggled up next to Dina to keep warm in the chill night air. He remembered being frightened by the vastness of the dark sky above, perforated by ten thousand sparkles of light. He could never get the image of endless space clear in his mind. His imaginary spaceship kept flying back into blue sky.

He had to keep reminding himself that the image was wrong, that black space didn't end, it kept going on... and on. Why did that frighten him so then?

He didn't know, but the images were so swift now that he couldn't linger long on any one of them, and the melancholy increased.

So this was the end. He'd probably never drive these roads again. Already they looked different in the moonlight, vague and unfamiliar, silvery shadows standing out from behind a tree or rock ledge. Whispers, echoes of other times and people, slipping away into the darkness. Just then Maggie stirred, coughed, and his thoughts returned to the joy she'd have in a few minutes. Indescribable warmth filled his heart and the goblins of gloom whisked away in the red afterglow of the taillights.

Soon he was driving up a four-lane highway and could already see the radiance of their destination rising from behind the hills. Ten more minutes and Maggie would have her wish. He pulled off at last onto a winding mountain road that he almost could've driven without his van lights on. The reflection of the illumination so bright against the sky, and his memories of the road so vivid.

He paused and turned down the purring heater—Maggie was sound asleep. He wanted so much to surprise her and keeping her eyes shut was vital. He hoped the growing roar as they grew closer to their destination wouldn't wake her until the last minute.

Finally, he eased to a stop in a parking area. There was a brilliance like daylight now and as he shut off the engine, the jet-like roar from outside the van was certain to rouse his daughter. She continued sleeping.

He stepped out, opened the door, and tapped her shoulder. "Magpie… it's Daddy. We've arrived at our destination. Wake up and remember to keep your eyes closed."

The little one roused, nodding her compliance. But a worried look caught Tommy's attention.

"Magpie? Are you okay? You look frightened."

"It's the noise, Daddy. What is that awful sound?"

"That," he said, lifting her from her seat, "is part of the surprise. Now keep your eyes shut, remember, for a few more minutes."

"I promise," she replied with a tremor in his voice. Tommy grabbed the gift and began to walk gingerly along an icy path. She buried her face in his chest as he carried her through the noise.

He made his way toward a glass paneled door. As he reached the entry it opened and a face he'd never seen, yet undeniably familiar, smiled.

"Mr. Howell, I presume." Tommy nodded. "I'm Bethany, Richard's sister."

Tommy stood Maggie on the floor, with another reminder about her eyes. "Hi, Bethany. I don't think I would have needed the intro. You look so much like Rick. This is Maggie."

Bethany knelt down and tapped Maggie's shoulder. "Hello Maggie."

"Hello," Maggie seemed more relaxed. The door had closed, and the roar diminished.

"Are you ready for your surprise?" Tommy took her hand. "Okay, keep your eyes closed for just a few minutes more."

Tommy followed Bethany as she led them up a flight of stairs and then crossed a carpeted area. Finally, she stopped, and Tommy felt a sense of elation.

He nodded at his host. "This is perfect Bethany. Thanks so much for your help. And now Maggie, off with your coat and then… open your eyes."

Tommy stepped away from his daughter so that he could catch the expected rapture in her eyes—he wasn't disappointed—she opened them and gasped. She was standing before a glass wall, next to a sparkling Christmas tree that towered above her for twenty feet. Beyond the glass was a large deck area covered—her eyes widened—with piles and piles of snow. Beyond the deck the hills were covered as sparkling icy flakes filled the air.

She dashed from point to point as Tommy watched, almost on the verge of tears.

"Daddy," she exclaimed. "It's snow. Snow—but how," she asked, finger on her lips. "Where are we?"

Laughing, he knelt down beside her. "This is Angel Valley, Magpie. It's a ski resort and they make snow here all winter long. The noise that scared you is those long pipes out there that spray water into the air. They're snowmaking machines."

"Daddy." She gasped. "Can we play in it?"

"We can, but only for a minute or two in these clothes, if you're not too cold."

She shook her head then dashed for the door, Tommy trailing behind and trying to get her to slow down long enough to put her coat on once more. Outside on the deck they made snowballs and a small snowman before going in again for her present, some sugar cookies, and cocoa. The excitement of the moment had overshadowed the idea of unwrapping the gift.

"Daddy, can we take this back home for tomorrow?"

"Of course, if that's what you want."

She nodded and nibbled, varying her glances from the tree to the sparkling slopes beyond the window.

"I can't thank you enough for taking the time to help me out like this, Bethany."

"I was more than glad to. You probably didn't know that our father used to bring us here when we were kids. I've so many fond memories of those times that I decided this was where I wanted to work. It's like home to me."

"I hope this will be a special memory as well."

"Yes," Bethany replied. "Yes, this will be an exceptional one."

They talked of many things for the next moments, and soon Maggie was winding down.

Tommy watched her little head bobbing back and forth as she valiantly tried to stay awake. At last her frame slumped over, and she slipped into deep sleep.

"Sweet thing. She's worn out." Tommy started putting her coat back on. "Could you do one more favor for me and help me get her to the car?"

"I'd be glad to." Bethany grabbed the unopened package and led the way to the van where Tommy strapped Maggie into her seat, shook hands with his new friend, and drove away destined for the very last Christmas at home.

Chapter Twenty

Maggie was sound asleep on the return drive, and no wonder. It was almost one-thirty before Tommy had her ready to slip beneath the covers once more. He thought he'd accomplish the task without waking her, but as he leaned over to kiss that precious forehead, she stirred.

"I love you, Magpie," he whispered.

"I love you too, Daddy."

Tommy pushed up when suddenly she whispered again.

"Daddy, I'm very proud of you." She turned and was asleep. Tommy was frozen.

Proud of you.

Why should three little words be so important? He didn't know, but they were. He thought about that first request Sherry had put to him: *If there is one thing you could know what would that be?* He'd found the solution to why Jesse hadn't kept his fishing trip promise. An answer that brought Tommy anger and anguish. Perhaps he should have asked for a different thing. Possibly he should have asked to know whether his father was ever proud of him. He pulled the door softly shut, resigned to the fact that he'd never know.

He shuffled quietly back to the living room where the box with Jesse's letters was still sitting on the table. They'd explored it together for an hour or so earlier that evening before the others had gone to bed, and he'd forgotten to close the container.

He sat down and began sorting the papers to put them away when one fell to the floor. Reaching down, he saw another paper lying folded beside it. He grabbed them both and laid them on the table. He rubbed his eyes and yawned. Morning was going to come very early, and he should hit the sack.

He grabbed the two letters to place them with the others, then noticed one was significantly different. The paper wasn't as old, the writing visibly worse. He opened the note and gasped, his eyes narrowing as he saw it was dated a year earlier. In his father's barely legible scrawl he read:

Tommy,

I failed you in a lot of ways, too many to list in my state of health. You may remember none of them, you may remember all. Before I die, I want to tell you what I never said and should have. I'm proud of you...

Tommy groaned audibly, the paper shaking in his hands. The writing even more illegible through the haze of tears.

I think you are a great father, a good husband... everything I never was. I'm very proud of you.

I've made my peace with God and ... I love you son,

There were no words, only tears—sweet, wonderful, liberating tears. Tommy sat in the darkness crying—laughing, a bundle of ecstasy where only grief had been. There were still many unanswered questions. But they paled now in the light of affirmation and love.

Things, frightful events come out of the dark times of life. But a father's love will always sustain.

When the crying was done Tommy sat for a while, wondering at the grace that allowed him to find the letters and the love behind them. Finally, he rose to put some wood in the fire, then went to the window to look once more on Destiny and gasped.

It was snowing.

Made in the USA
Middletown, DE
26 September 2024

61039391R00091